The High School Boys' Training Hike

Making Themselves "Hard as Nails"

H. Irving Hancock

1st WORLD
LIBRARY
Literary Society

The High School Boys' Training Hike

H. Irving Hancock

© 1st World Library – Literary Society, 2005
PO Box 2211
Fairfield, IA 52556
www.1stworldlibrary.org
First Edition

LCCN: 2004195629

Softcover ISBN: 1-4218-0450-6
Hardcover ISBN: 1-4218-0350-X
eBook ISBN: 1-4218-0550-2

Purchase *"The High School Boys' Training Hike"*
as a traditional bound book at:
www.1stWorldLibrary.org/purchase.asp?ISBN=1-4218-0450-6

1st World Library Literary Society is a nonprofit
organization dedicated to promoting literacy by:

- Creating a free internet library accessible from any
  computer worldwide.
- Hosting writing competitions and offering book
  publishing scholarships.

The High School Boys' Training Hike
contributed by Tim, Ed & Rodney
in support of
1st World Library Literary Society

CONTENTS

CHAPTER I

MR. TITMOUSE DOESN'T KNOW DICK

"We thought ten dollars would be about right," Dick Prescott announced.

"Per week?" inquired Mr. Titmouse, as though he doubted his hearing.

"Oh, dear, no! For the month of August, sir."

Mr. Newbegin Titmouse surveyed his young caller through half-closed eyelids.

"Ten dollars for the use of that fine wagon for a whole month?" cried Mr. Titmouse in astonishment. "Absurd!"

"Very likely I am looking at it from the wrong point of view," admitted Prescott, who fingered a ten dollar bill and was slowly smoothing it out so that Mr. Titmouse might see it.

"That wagon was put together especially for the purpose," Mr. Titmouse resumed. "It has seats that run lengthwise, and eight small cupboards and lockers under the seats. There is a place to secure the cook stove at the rear end of the wagon, and the stove rests on zinc. Though the wagon is light enough for one horse to draw it, it will hold all that several people could require for camping or for leading a regular gipsy life. There is a special awning that covers the wagon when needed, so that on a rainy day you can travel without using umbrellas or getting wet. You can cook equally well on the stove whether in camp or on the road. There are not many vehicles in which you can cook a full meal when traveling from one point to another."

"Nor is it every stewpan or kettle that would refrain from slipping off the stove when driving the wagon over rough roads," laughed Dick good-humoredly.

"Well - er - of course, one has to choose decent roads when touring with a wagon of that sort," admitted the owner.

"Then you don't think ten dollars a fair price?" Dick Prescott inquired thoughtfully.

"For a month's use of the wagon? I do not," replied Mr. Newbegin Titmouse with emphasis.

"And so you decline our offer of ten dollars?" Prescott asked, looking still more thoughtful.

"I certainly do," replied Mr. Titmouse.

Then the owner of the wagon began to descant glowingly upon the many advantages of going on a road hike aided by the service that such a specially constructed wagon would give. In fact, Mr. Titmouse dwelt so enthusiastically upon the value of his wagon that Dick shrewdly told himself:

H. Irving Hancock

"He's very anxious - unusually so - to rent us that wagon. I've already found out that he hasn't used the wagon in two years, nor has he succeeded in renting it to anyone else. The wagon is so much useless lumber in his stable."

"I wouldn't rent that wagon to everyone," Mr. Titmouse wound up.

"No, sir," Dick agreed heartily, yet with a most innocent look in his face. "Not everyone would want the wagon."

"I - I don't mean that!" Mr. Titmouse exclaimed.

"In fact, sir," Dick went on very smoothly, "I have learned that you have been offering the wagon for sale or hire during the last two summers, without getting any customers."

"Eh?" demanded Mr. Titmouse in some astonishment.

"Naturally, sir," Dick went on, "before coming here to see you I made a few inquiries in Tottenville. I discovered that in this vicinity the wagon is something of a joke."

"What's that?" questioned the other sharply. "My camping wagon a joke? Nothing of the sort. And, if it is a joke, why did you want to get it?"

"Oh, all of our fellows can stand a joke," laughed young Prescott "So I came over to see just what terms we could make for the use of your wagon during the month of August."

"Well, I'll be as fair with you as I can," Mr. Titmouse replied. "From men - grown men - I would want at least thirty dollars a month for the wagon - probably thirty-five. Of course I know that money is not as plentiful with boys. I'll let you have the wagon for the month of August at the bottom price of twenty-five dollars."

Dick smilingly shook his head.

"I've named the best price I could think of taking," insisted Mr. Titmouse. "Come into the wagon shed and have another look at it."

"Thank you, sir, but there is no use in looking at the wagon again, when such a price as twenty-five dollars is asked for a month's hire," Dick answered promptly.

"Come inside and look at it again, anyway," urged Mr. Titmouse.

"Thank you, sir, but I must get back to Gridley at the earliest possible moment."

"If you didn't want to hire the wagon," asked Mr. Titmouse testily, "what was the use of taking up my time?"

"I do want to hire it," Dick admitted, "but since hearing your price I have realized that I don't want the wagon half as much as I did at the outset."

It was notable about Mr. Titmouse that he would gladly talk for three hours in order to gain a dollar's advantage in any trade in which he was interested. He was a small man, with small features and very small eyes which, somehow, suggested gimlets. He bore about with him always an air of injury, as though deeply sensitive over the supposed fact that the whole world was concerned in getting the better of him.

Though Mr. Titmouse had acquired, through sharp dealing, usury and in many other ways a considerable sum of money and property in the course of his life, yet he was not the man to part with any of it needlessly.

The special wagon now resting in the wagon shed at his home place in Tottenville had been designed by him at a time when people all through the state had been much interested in outdoor life. The Titmouse wagon had been built as the result of much thought on the part of its designer. It certainly was a handy kind of wagon for campers to use on the road. Mr. Titmouse had spent four weeks of wandering life, going from point to point and trying to talk up the merits of his wagon. He had hoped to establish a small factory, there to build such wagons to order at high prices.

For some reason he had met with no success in that enterprise. After his realization of failure Newbegin Titmouse had felt that he would be content if he could sell the wagon at anything like a good price. Failing to sell it, he hoped to be able to get his money back through renting the wagon.

Now he stood watching this high school boy from Gridley, wondering just how much rental he could extort from this wiry, athletic-looking football player.

"There will be a car along in about five minutes," mused Dick aloud. "I must try to take that car. Thank you very much for your kindness, Mr. Titmouse."

"But we haven't come to any understanding yet," cried the wagon's owner as Dick turned and walked away.

"Why, yes, we have, sir," Prescott answered pleasantly over his shoulder. "We have come to the understanding that you can't afford to come down to our price, and that we can't go up to yours. So I'm going back to make some other arrangements for a wagon."

"Wait a minute!" interjected Newbegin Titmouse, stepping after the boy from Gridley. "Maybe I can drop off a dollar or so on the price."

"Much obliged, sir; but it wouldn't help us any, and it's almost time for the car," was Prescott's answer.

"What's your best offer? Make it!" urged Mr. Titmouse restlessly.

"Seven dollars for the wagon for the month of August," Prescott replied.

"Seven? Why, only a minute or two ago you offered me ten dollars!"

"I know it, sir," said Dick coolly. "You will recall that you declined that offer, so I am at liberty to make a new offer."

"You'll have to make a better -"

"If you decline seven dollars," Dick smiled pleasantly, "my next offer, if I make one, will not go above six."

Mr. Titmouse felt, of a sudden, very certain that the high school boy would stand by that threat.

"Seven dollars doesn't land me clear for the season," complained Newbegin Titmouse. "I've spent nine dollars already in advertising the wagon."

"Then, if you don't take my seven dollars," Prescott proposed, "you'll be out quite a bit of money, Mr. Titmouse. I see my car coming in the distance. So good -"

"I'll take ten!" called Mr. Titmouse, as Dick once more turned away.

"Six," smiled Dick significantly. "But I haven't time to stay here and dicker, sir. Good -"

"Hold on!" fairly screamed Mr. Titmouse, as Dick, nodding at him, started to run to the corner.

"Then I'll stop and talk it over with you, sir," answered Prescott, going back. "But I don't say that I'll agree to take the wagon."

"Now, don't you try to work the price down any lower," exclaimed Mr. Titmouse, looking worried.

"No, sir; I won't do that," Dick promised. "I won't say, yet, that I'll take the wagon, but I will agree that I'll either take it at six dollars or refuse the chance altogether. I've just happened to think of something that I want to make sure about"

"What is it?" asked Mr. Titmouse apprehensively.

"I forgot to look at the tires on the wheels," Prescott went on. "I want to make sure that they're sound, so that we fellows won't have to take the chance of paying a blacksmith to make new ones before we've been out a week."

The tires were in excellent condition, so the little man had no objection whatever to showing them.

"Good, so far," nodded Prescott. "Now, next, I'd enjoy looking at the axles and the hub-nuts."

"You're not the lad who is going to allow himself to be cheated," laughed Mr. Titmouse admiringly. "The hubs and axles are all right, so I've no objection to showing them to you."

"I'm satisfied with the wagon," Dick declared, a few minutes later. "Now, Mr. Titmouse, I'll pay you the six dollars if you'll make out a satisfactory receipt for the money."

"Come into the office and tell me what you want me to say in the receipt," urged Newbegin Titmouse, leading the way across the stable into a little room in the furthermost corner.

The receipt was soon made out, the money paid and the receipt in Dick's pocket.

"I'll either come for the wagon myself, or send one of the other fellows," Dick promised. "If I send for it I'll also send a written order."

"I hope you boys will have a pleasant time this summer," chirped Mr. Titmouse, who, though he had been badly out-generaled in the trade, had at least the satisfaction of knowing that there was some money in his pocket that had come to him by sheer good luck.

"We're going to try to have the finest good time that a crowd of fellows ever had," Dick replied, after nodding his thanks. "I've missed that car, and shall have quite a little wait."

"Perhaps you'd like to sit under a tree and eat a few apples," suggested Mr. Titmouse.

Dick was about to accept the invitation with thanks when Mr. Titmouse added:

"I've a lot of fine summer apples I gathered yesterday. I'll let you have three for five cents."

This attempt at petty trade, almost in the guise of hospitality, struck Dick as being so utterly funny that he could not help laughing outright.

"Thank you, Mr. Titmouse," he replied. "I don't believe I'll eat any apples just now."

"I might make it four for a nickel," coaxed the little man, "if you agree not to pick out the largest apples."

"Thank you, but I don't believe I'll eat any apples at all just now," Dick managed to reply, then made his escape in time to avoid laughing in Mr. Titmouse's face.

Once out on the street, and knowing that he had some twenty minutes to wait for the next car, Dick strolled slowly along.

"I didn't know that boy," muttered Newbegin Titmouse, looking after Prescott with a half admiring gaze, "and I didn't size him up right. He offered me ten dollars, and then got the wagon for six. Whew! I don't believe I ever before got off so badly as that in a trade. But I really did spend five-fifty in advertising the wagon in the Tottenville and Gridley papers this summer, so I'm fifty cents ahead, anyway, and a fifty-cent piece is always equivalent to half a dollar!"

With which sage reflection Mr. Newbegin Titmouse went out into his small orchard to see whether he had overlooked any summer apples that were worth two dollars a barrel.

Dick sauntered down the street for a few blocks ere he heard the whirr of a Gridley-bound trolley car behind him. He quickened his pace until he reached the next corner. There he signaled to the motorman.

As the car slowed down Dick swung himself on nimbly, remarking to the conductor:

"Don't make a real stop for me. Drive on!"

As Prescott passed inside the car he was greeted by a pleasant-faced, well-dressed young man. It was Mr. Luce, one of the sub-masters of Gridley High School. Dick dropped into a seat beside him.

"Been tramping a bit, Prescott?" inquired the sub-master.

"No, sir; I've been over here on a little matter of business, but I expect to start, in a day or two, on a few weeks of tramping."

Thereupon young Prescott fell to describing the trip that he, Dave Darrin, Greg Holmes, Dan Dalzell, Tom Reade and Harry Hazelton had mapped out for themselves.

"Just for pleasure?" asked Mr. Luce.

"No, sir; for training. We all hope to make the football team this fall. We're all of us in pretty good shape, too, I think, sir; but we're going out on this training hike to see if we can't work ourselves down as hard as nails."

"I'd like to go with you," nodded the sub-master.

"Can't you do it, sir?" asked Dick eagerly, for Mr. Luce was a favorite with all the boys.

"Unfortunately, I can't," replied the submaster. "I'm expected at home. My mother and sister claim me for this month. But I wish I could go, just the same."

"You would be most welcome I assure you, sir," replied Dick warmly.

"Thank you, Prescott," returned Mr. Luce with a smile. "I appreciate your invitation and regret that I cannot accept it."

The conversation again turned to the subject of the coming football season, and an animated discussion ensued, as Sub-master Luce was an enthusiastic advocate of football.

Suddenly, Dick, glancing ahead out of the window, turned pale. Without a word of explanation he sprang from his seat and made a bound for the nearer car door, the rear one.

"Everyone off! Stop the car! Hustle!" shouted the high school boy. "Mr. Luce! Come on. Quick!"

By the time the last words were uttered Dick had made a flying leap from the car platform.

By good luck, rather more than by expert work, he landed on his feet. Not an instant did he lose, but dashed along at full speed.

John Luce, though he had no inkling of what had caused the excitement, sprang after Dick.

Dick, however, had not waited to see if the sub-master had followed him. His horror-filled eyes, as he ran, were turned straight ahead.

It needed but a few steps to carry him across the road. He bounded into a field where a loaded hay wagon stood near an apple tree.

The horses had been led away to be fed. Seated on the top of the hay were a boy of barely six and a girl not more than four years old. They were awaiting the return of the farmer.

Down below a six-year-old boy, barefooted and brown as a gipsy, had appeared on the scene during the farmer's absence.

"For fun" this youngster had been lighting match after match, making believe to set the hay afire. As he held the matches as close to the dried hay as he dared, this urchin on the ground called to the two babies above that he would "burn 'em up."

Not all of this did Dick Prescott know, but his glance through the car window had shown him the boy on the ground just as that tiny fellow had lighted another match, shouting tantalizingly to the two children on top of the load of hay.

Just as he called up to them the mischievous youngster tripped slightly. Throwing out his right hand to save himself the boy accidentally touched the bottom of the load at one side with the lighted match.

At this fateful instant it was out of the question to think of putting out the flame that leaped from wisp to wisp of the dried grass.

"Jump!" shouted the young match-burner, but the children above did not hear, or else did not realize their plight.

"Fire! Fire!" screamed the little incendiary, as he ran panic-stricken toward the farm house.

And now Dick was racing as he had never done before, even over the football gridiron. On his speed depended the lives of the two children.

CHAPTER II

THE DEED OF A HERO

At the moment of Dick's leap from the car, Sub-master Luce did not know what had happened. He realized in an instant what was the matter, and made frantic efforts to reach the scene at the same moment with Prescott.

Dick, however, kept the lead.

As the flames shot up through the hay the children on top of the hay began to gather a sense of their awful danger.

Seconds - fractions of seconds - were of priceless value now - if lives were to be saved.

There was still time for the two children to jump over the side on which the flames had not yet appeared, but they were too badly frightened to know what to do.

If they should jump where the flames were leaping up they were almost certain to have their clothing catch fire, with fatal burns as a result.

Dick felt that he did not have time to shout to the frightened children. Besides, his commands would

H. Irving Hancock

likely serve only to confuse them the more.

Terror-stricken the two little ones clasped each other and stood screaming with fear on the top of the load.

Dick's quick eye had taken in the only chance in this terrifying situation.

Straight for the apple tree he bounded, his first leap carrying him into a crotch in the tree a few feet above the ground.

Out he sprang, now, on a limb of the tree that most nearly overhung the load of hay.

That limb sagged under him - creaked - threatened to snap off under his weight.

But young Prescott, wholly heedless of his own safety, and with only one object in mind, scrambled out on the creaking limb as far as he could; then, with a prayer on his lips, he made a wild, strenuous leap.

Sub-master Luce turned white as he saw what Dick had attempted to do. Had he been made of more timorous stuff the high school teacher would have closed his eyes for that awful instant.

As it was, John Luce saw young Prescott land at the rear end of the load.

Dick felt himself slipping. For one frenzied second, he feared that he had failed. Young Strongheart that he was, he braced all his muscles for the supreme effort - and drew himself up to safer footing on the hay.

Then, like an eagle, he swooped down upon the children. The little girl he snatched from her tiny brother's clasp.

"Here!" called Sub-master Luce from the further side.

Brief as the time was Dick Prescott calculated the distance like lightning. There was no time to call back to Mr. Lucen - nor need to do so.

Aiming with all the precision at his command, Dick threw the child from him.

His aim splendidly true, he had the joy of seeing the child land in Mr. Luce's arms.

Without a moment's loss of time Prescott now snatched up the shrieking boy.

"Ready!" shouted Dick, and a second little body was thrown through the air.

Again did John Luce do credit to his college baseball training, for, hurriedly placing the girl baby on the ground he put up his hands to receive the boy.

"Jump yourself, Prescott!" bawled the submaster hoarsely.

But Dick was already in the air. With the flames shooting up and seeming fairly to lick his face, Dick had had no time to calculate his jump.

On the ground, some feet beyond the wagon, Prescott landed, sprawling on all fours.

He leaped up, however, his face twitching yet with a laugh on his lips.

Behind him the whole load of hay now flared up, crackling and hissing.

"Hurry back out of the heat!" yelled John Luce, leaping forward, seizing young Prescott and dragging him several yards away.

Dick turned in time to see the whole glowing mass cave in.

Had he arrived on the scene a few seconds later than he did both children would have perished miserably.

Now, from the house came a white-faced man, running as though some demon animated him. Behind him came a woman even paler.

Toward father and mother ran the pair of little tots, wholly unmindful of their rescuers.

As for the older, match-burning boy, that youngster half scared to death, had dashed away into hiding to escape the wrath that he knew must soon seek him.

"That was simply magnificent, Prescott!" said the sub-master enthusiastically. "But I honestly believed that it would be your last good deed."

While the sub-master spoke he was running both hands up and down over the high school boy's clothing, putting out many glowing sparks that had found lodgment in the cloth.

"It was easy," smiled Dick. "Thank goodness I saw the trouble in time!"

"There are others who are thankful that you saw it in time," uttered John Luce, as he looked toward the parents, now coming up as fast as they could, each with a child clasped in arms.

From the road went up a loud cheer. The trolley car had been halted and backed down to the scene. Though there were few people on the car, they made up amply in enthusiasm for their lack of numbers.

As for the farmer and his wife, though they tried to thank Dick and Mr. Luce, they were too completely overcome with emotion to express themselves intelligibly.

The wagon that had held the hay was now blazing fiercely. As for the hay, that had already burned to a fine powder.

"How - how did you ever get here in time?" cried the rejoicing mother brokenly.

It was the conductor of the trolley car, just reaching the spot, who told how Dick Prescott and Mr. Luce had leaped from the moving car. The sub-master described Dick's feat in climbing the apple tree and leaping from the limb of the tree to the top of the loaded hay wagon.

"It was a nervy thing for any man to do!" choked the farmer, tears of joy running down his cheeks.

"It was just like Dick Prescott," replied John Luce simply.

As soon as possible Dick and the sub-master made their escape from the earnest protestations of gratitude of the farmer and his wife, though they did not go until Mr. Luce had persuaded the parents not to whip the mischievous match-burner, but to content themselves with pointing out to the little rascal the dreadful possibilities of such pranks.

At last, however, Dick and Mr. Luce returned to the car followed by the other passengers. The conductor gave the go-ahead signal, and the motor-man started in to try to make up some of the time lost from his schedule.

Dick, as soon as he reached Gridley, went up to Greg Holmes' house, where he knew his chums would be waiting to learn the result of his Tottenville trip.

That evening Sub-master Luce chanced to take a stroll up Main Street. As the offices of the "Morning Blade" were lighted up, Mr. Luce stepped inside, seeking Editor Pollock in the editorial room.

"Is Prescott about?" asked Mr. Luce, for Dick, as our readers know, earned many a dollar as a "space-writer"; that is, he was paid so much a column for furnishing and writing up local news.

"Dick went out about ten minutes ago," replied Mr. Pollock.

"Was he here long?"

"About fifteen minutes."

"By the way, Mr. Pollock," the sub-master went on,

"what do you think of Dick's latest feat?"

"Which one?"

"His fine work over on the Tottenville road this afternoon?"

"I haven't heard of it," replied Mr. Pollock, opening his eyes.

"Come to think of it," rejoined John Luce, "and knowing young Prescott as I do, I don't suppose you have heard of it - not from Prescott, at all events."

Then the sub-master told the story of the burning load of hay in a way that made the "Blade's" editor reach hastily for pencil and paper that he might take notes.

"That's just the kind of story that Dick Prescott never could be depended upon to bring in here - if he was the central character in it," observed the editor quietly.

Despite the failure of Dick to bring in this particular story, however, the "Blade," the next morning, printed more than a column from the data furnished by Mr. Luce.

Dick, however, didn't hear of it - -in Gridley. It was Harry Hazelton, who, at four o'clock, mounted a horse he had hired for the trip and rode over to Tottenville, where the camp wagon was obtained from Mr. Newbegin Titmouse. Hazelton wasted no time on the road, but drove as fast as the horse could comfortably travel.

It was but a few minutes after six o'clock, that August

morning, when Dick Prescott and his five chums, collectively famous as Dick & Co., drove out of Gridley.

Harry Hazelton was now the driver, the other five high school boys walking briskly just ahead of the wagon.

Mr. Titmouse's special vehicle carried all that Dick & Co. would need in the near future, and the six boys were setting out on what was destined to be their most famous vacation jaunt.

CHAPTER III

THE PEDDLER AND THE LAWYER'S HALF

Just before leaving Gridley, Greg Holmes had bought a copy of the "Blade" from a newsboy.

Three miles out, the chums enjoyed their first halt.

"Ten minutes' rest under this tree," Dick announced, for already the August morning sun was beating down upon them.

Greg drew out his copy of the newspaper, unfolding it.

"Say!" he yelled suddenly.

"Stop that," commanded Tom Reade, "or you'll make the horse run away and wreck our outfit."

"But this paper says -"

"Stop it," ordered Tom with a scowl. "I know what you're going to do. You'll read us some exciting stuff, and get us all worked up, and then in the last paragraph you'll stumble on the fact that some well-known Tottenville man was cured of all his ailments by Brown's Blood Bitters."

H. Irving Hancock

"Can you hold your tongue a minute?" demanded Greg ironically.

"Not when I see you headed that way," retorted Reade. "I've been fooled by the same style of exciting item, and I know how cheap it makes a fellow feel when he comes to the name of the Bitters, the Pills or the Sarsaparilla. Holmesy, I want to save your face for you with this crowd."

"Will you keep quiet, for a moment, and let the other fellows hear, even if you have to take a walk in order to save your own ears?" demanded Greg, with sarcasm. "This piece is about Dick Prescott, and he doesn't sign patent medicine test -"

"Dick Prescott?" demanded Darrin. "Whoop! Let's have it!"

"It isn't a roast, is it?" demanded Danny Grin solemnly.

"No; it isn't," Greg went on. "Listen, while I read the headlines."

It was a four-line heading, beginning with "Dick Prescott's Fine Nerve."

"There! I was afraid it was a roast, after all," sighed Danny Grin.

"Take that fellow away and muzzle him," ordered Greg, then proceeded to read the other sections of the headlines.

By this time Greg had a very attentive audience. Even Tom Reade had ceased to scoff.

"Oh, bosh!" gasped Dick, when Greg was about one third of the way through the column article.

"Isn't it true?" demanded Dave.

"After a fashion," Dick admitted.

"Then hold off and be good while the rest of us hear about yesterday's doings."

So Dick stood by, his face growing redder and redder as the reading proceeded.

"That's what I call a dandy story," declared Greg as he finished reading.

"Dick, why didn't you tell us something about it last night?" demanded Hazelton.

"What was the use?" asked Prescott. "And, though I've always thought the 'Blade' a fine local newspaper, I don't quite approve of Mr. Pollock's judgment of news values in this instance. I suspect that Mr. Pollock must have been away, and that Mr. Bradley, the news editor, ran this in."

"It sounds like some of Len Spencer's stuff," guessed Dave. "He's great on local events."

"If they had to print the yarn, eight or ten lines would have covered it," Dick declared. "Fellows, we've used up eighteen minutes for our halt, instead of ten. Come on!"

Greg, however, after rising, and before starting, was careful to fold the "Blade" neatly and to tuck it away in a pocket. He meant to save that news story.

All of our readers are familiar with the lives and doings of Dick Prescott and his friends up to date.

"Dick & Co.," as the boys styled their unorganized club of chums, was made up of the six boys, who had been fast friends back in their days of study at the Central Grammar School of Gridley.

They had been together in everything, and notably so in athletics and sports. All that befell them in their later days at Central Grammar School is told fully in the four volumes of the "*Grammar School Boys Series.*"

Yet it was when these same boys entered Gridley High School that they came into the fullest measure of their local fame and popularity. Even as freshmen they found a chance to accomplish far more for school athletics than is usually permitted to freshmen. It was due to their efforts that athletics were put on a sound financial basis in the Gridley High School. All this and more is described in the first volume of the "*High School Boys Series,*" entitled "*The High School Freshmen.*"

But it was in the second volume of that series, "*The High School Pitcher,*" that our readers found Dick & Co. entered fully in the training squads of one of the most famous of American high schools. As described in the third volume, "*The High School Left End,*" Dick & Co. were transferred from the baseball nine to the gridiron eleven, and by this time had become the undisputed athletic leaders of Gridley High School. These honors they had not won without tremendous opposition, especially by the formation of the notorious "Sorehead Squad" to oppose their hard earned supremacy in football. Yet Dick & Co. ever went strenuously forward, in manly, clean-cut fashion, working unceasingly for the furthering of honest American sport. Between the plottings of their enemies and a host of adventures on all sides, the school life of Dick & Co. proved exciting indeed.

In the "*High School Boys' Vacation Series*" our readers have followed the summer doings of Dick & Co. as distinguished from the doings of their crowded school years. The first volume devoted to the vacations of Dick & Co., "*The High School Boys' Canoe Club*," describes the adventures of our lads in an Indian war canoe which even their slender financial resources enabled them to buy at an auction sale of the effects of a stranded Wild West Show. In the second volume of this series, "*The High School Boys In Summer Camp*," our readers came upon an even more exciting narrative of keenly enjoyed summer doings, replete with lively adventures. In that volume the activities of Tag Mosher, a strangely odd character, kept Dick & Co. continually on the alert. In the third volume of the vacation series, entitled "*The High School Boys' Fishing Trip*," were chronicled the things that befell Dick & Co. while away on a fishing expedition that became famous in the annals of Gridley school days. This third volume was full to the brim with the sort of adventures that boys most love. Some old enemies of Dick & Co. appeared; how they were put to rout is well known to all our readers. How Dick & Co. played a huge joke, and several smaller ones upon their enemies, is described in that volume.

In this present volume will be recounted all that befell Dick & Co. in August after completing their junior year in Gridley High School, just as the preceding or third volume dealt with the happenings of July of that same summer.

After that first halt Dick & Co. plodded on for another hour. But Prescott, noting that Hazelton was still on the driver's seat of the camp wagon, blandly inquired:

"Harry, if you sit up there, lazily holding the reins, how do you expect to get your share of the training work of this hike?"

"Perhaps I'd rather have the comfort than the training work," laughed Hazelton.

"That will never do!" smiled Dick. "Suppose you climb down and let Danny Grin take your place at the reins until the next halt. I suspect that Danny boy already has a few pebbles in his shoes, and that he'll be glad enough to look over the world from the driver's seat."

"I'm willing to sacrifice myself for the good of the expedition, anyway," sighed Dalzell, as Harry drew rein. "Come down with you, Hazy, and begin to share the delights of this walking match!"

The change of drivers made, Dick & Co. plodded on again.

"It seems to me that we ought to put on more speed," suggested Dave Darrin.

"Are you in a hurry to get somewhere, Darry?" drawled Tom Reade.

"No," Dave replied, "but, if we're out for training, it

seems to me that we had better do brisker walking than we're doing now, even if the horse can't keep up with us."

"We're making about three miles and a half an hour," Dick responded.

"But will that be work enough to make us as hard as nails?" persisted Darry.

"We're getting over the ground as fast as the troops of the regular army usually travel," Prescott rejoined. "I believe our regulars are generally regarded as rather perfect specimens in the walking line. We might move along at a speed of six miles, and might keep it up for an hour. Then we'd be footsore, and all in. If the first hour didn't do it, the second hour would. But if we plug along in this deliberate fashion, and get over fifteen, eighteen or twenty miles a day, and keep it up, I don't believe any one of you fellows will complain, September first, that he isn't as hard and solid as he wants to be - even for bucking the football lines, of other high schools."

"I know that I can be satisfied with this gait," murmured Reade.

"If Darry wants to move faster," suggested Hazelton, "why not tell him where to wait for us, and let him gallop ahead?"

"I'll stay with the rest of you," Darry retorted. "All I want to make sure of is that we're going to get the most out of our training work this summer."

"I'll tell you what you might do, Dave, by way of extra

exercise and hardening," offered Tom.

"What?" asked Dave suspiciously.

"I believe we're going to halt every hour for a brief rest"

"Yes."

"While the five of us are resting under the trees, Darry, you might climb the trees, swinging from limb to limb and leaping from tree to tree. Of course you'll select trees that are not directly over our heads."

"Humph!" retorted Dave.

"Try it, anyway," urged Tom, "it's fine exercise, even if you give it up after a while."

"I'll try it as often as you do," Darrin agreed with a grin.

Their second halt found the high school boys more than six miles from their starting point.

On this trip they were not heading in the direction they had followed on their fishing trip. Instead, they were traveling in the opposite direction from Gridley, through a fairly populous farming region.

At a quarter-past ten o'clock Dick called for another halt. The road map that the boys had brought along showed them that they were now eleven miles from Gridley.

"Pretty fair work," muttered Tom, "considering that

these roads were built by men who had never seen any better kind."

"We can more than double the distance," suggested Dave, "before we go into camp for the night."

"If we hike a couple more miles this morning, then halt, get the noon meal and rest until two o'clock," replied young Prescott, "I think we shall do better."

"If we've gone only eleven miles," protested Darrin, "then I'm certainly good for twenty-five miles in all to-day, and I believe the rest of you are, too."

"Wait until we've done eighteen or twenty miles," Prescott proposed. "Then we can take a vote about making it twenty-five."

"For one thing," Darry objected, "none of us actually walks twenty-five miles when we cover that distance. We take turns riding on the wagon, and, as there are six of us, that means that each fellow rides something like four miles of the distance covered."

"What Darry is driving at," proposed Danny Grin, "is that he wants to devote himself wholly to walking hereafter. He doesn't care about driving the horse."

"I'm big enough and cranky enough to do my own talking, when there is any reason for my entering into the conversation," smiled Dave.

At a little after eleven that morning, when thirteen and a half miles had been covered, all hands were willing enough to halt and rest, prepare luncheon and rest again.

H. Irving Hancock

"But I still hope we shall cover the twenty-five miles to-day," Darry insisted.

"No difficulty about that, either," declared Harry Hazelton. "Darry, while we are swapping stories over the campfire this evening you can take a lantern and do an extra five miles by way of an evening walk. Then you'll be tired enough to sleep."

"I'll see about it," Darrin laughed.

"And that's the last we'll hear about it," Tom predicted dryly.

"It is the experience of every military commander, so I've read," Dick went on, "that a long march the first day of a big hike is no especially good sign of how the soldiers will hold out to the end. On the contrary, military men have found that it's better to march a shorter distance on the first day and to work up gradually to a good standard of performance."

"All right," agreed Hazelton. "For one, I'm willing to take a rest after eating, and then take the afternoon for getting acquainted with this pretty grove."

"We won't quite do that, either, if I have my way," Prescott laughed. "We ought to do a few miles this afternoon, but not set out to do any record-breaking or back-breaking stunt."

"There goes hazy's dream up in the air," laughed Greg. "I just knew that Hazy was planning how to spend the afternoon napping."

"I'll volunteer to drive all the way, this afternoon,"

Harry offered. "That will give all of you fellows a chance to harden yourselves more on the first day."

"If you want to know a good definition of 'generosity,' then ask Hazy," snorted Dalzell.

"Come on!" cried Dick good-humoredly. "Scatter. Some for wood, some for water. Tom and I will get the kitchen kit ready for a meal. But we must have the wood and water before we can prepare luncheon."

At that suggestion of something to eat there was a general rush to get things in readiness. As soon as a fire was going in the stove in the wagon, Dick put on a frying pan. Into this he dropped several slices of bacon. Tom, over a fire built on the ground, set the coffee-pot going. In a pot on the stove Dick put potatoes to cook.

Now Dave rattled out the dishes, as soon as Greg and Hazy had set up the folding table. Dan placed the chairs.

"Get ready!" called Dick, as soon as he had fried two platters full of bacon and eggs. Tom, will you try the potatoes?"

"Done," responded Reade, after prodding the potatoes with a fork.

"What shall we do with the food that's left over?" asked Danny Grin, as he began to eat.

"There isn't going to be any food left over," Dick laughed. "You fellows will be lucky, indeed, if you get as much as you want."

Everyone was satisfied, however, by the time that the meal was finished.

"Greg and Harry may have the pleasure of washing the dishes," Dick suggested.

"Oh, dear!" grunted Hazy, but he went at his task without further remarks.

Before one o'clock everything was in readiness for going forward again, save for putting the horse between the shafts of the wagon. Prescott, however, put a proposition to rest until two o'clock before his chums. It was unanimously carried.

Despite his desire for a walking record that day, Darry proved quite willing to lie off at full length in the shade of the trees and doze as much as the flies would permit.

Dick and Tom strolled slowly down toward the road, halting by a couple of trees.

"There's something you don't often see, nowadays," spoke up Tom after a while.

He nodded back up the road. Coming in the same direction that the boys themselves had traveled was a faded, queer-looking old red wagon, much decorated on the outside by a lot of hanging, swinging tin and agate ware.

"That's the old-fashioned tin-peddler that I've heard a good deal about as being a common enough character some forty years ago," said Prescott. "Our grandmothers used to save up meat-bones, rags and bottles and trade them off to the peddler, receiving tinware in return."

"The man on that wagon was doing business forty years ago," remarked Tom. "In fact, judging by his appearance, he must have been quite a veteran at the business even forty years ago."

A bent, little old man it was who was perched upon the seat of the red wagon. Once upon a time his hair had been tawny. Now it was streaked liberally with gray. He was smoking a black little wooden pipe and paying small attention to the sad-eyed, bony horse between the shafts. There was a far-away, rather dull look in the old peddler's eyes.

Just before he reached the boys, whom he had not seen, he took a piece of paper from his pocket, pulled his spectacles down from his forehead and read the paper.

"I don't understand it," muttered the peddler, aloud. "I can't understand it. I wish I had someone to give me the right of it."

"Could we be of any service, sir?" Reade inquired.

Hearing a human voice so close at hand the peddler started for an instant. Then he pulled in the horse.

"I dunno whether you can be of much use to me," answered the peddler slowly. "You don't look old enough to know much about business."

"Still, I know more than anyone would think, from just

looking at me," volunteered Reade, reddening a bit as he saw the laughter in Dick Prescott's eyes.

"Maybe you can explain this riddle," went on the peddler, extending the sheet of white paper. "It can't do any harm to give you a chance. You see, I had a bill of twenty dollars against Bill Peterson. The bill had been running three years, and I couldn't get anything out of Bill but promises without any exact dates tied to 'em. I needed the money as bad as Bill did, so at last I went to Lawyer Stark to see what could be done about it. Lawyer Stark said he'd tackle the job if I'd give him half. I agreed to that, for half a loaf is better'n nothing at all, as you may have heard. Then weeks went by, and I heard nothing from Squire Stark. So the other night I writ a letter, asking him how the collection of the bill was coming on. This is the answer he sends me."

So Tom read aloud, from the typewritten sheet, the following remarkably brief communication:

"Dear Sir: Answering your letter of yesterday's date, I have to advise you that I have collected my half of the Peterson bill. Your half I regard as extremely doubtful."

This was signed with the name of Lawyer Stark.

Tom Reade glanced through the note again, then gave vent to a shout of laughter.

"Eh?" asked the peddler looking puzzled.

"I beg your pardon, sir," replied Reade instantly. "I shouldn't have laughed, but this struck me, at first, as one of the funniest letters I ever saw. So the lawyer has collected his half of the twenty and regards the collection of your half as exceedingly doubtful!"

"Shouldn't Lawyer Stark give me half of the ten he got from Bill Peterson?" asked the peddler anxiously.

"Undoubtedly he should," Tom assented, "and just as undoubtedly he hasn't any idea of doing so."

"What do you say, young man?" inquired the peddler, turning to young Prescott.

"Why, sir, if you are asking about your legal chance of getting half of that ten dollars from the lawyer," Dick answered, "then I'm afraid you stand a poor show. If the lawyer won't pay you the money, then you would have to sue him. Even if you won the suit, the fight would cost you a good deal more than the amount you would recover. And the lawyer might beat you, even if you sued him."

"Then - what's the answer?" demanded the peddler slowly.

"I know the answer," said Tom confidently, "but it would be a shame to tell you, sir."

"Just the same, I wish you would," replied the peddler coaxingly.

"The answer," replied Reade, "is that you have been cheated."

"But it looks to me like a mean trick," Dick went on.

"What am I going to do about it?" asked the peddler wonderingly.

"I don't believe you can do anything about it, sir," Prescott answered, "unless you are willing to sue the lawyer, or can make him agree to fair play. But I certainly would drop in to see him and tell him that you expect just half of what he has so far collected."

"I believe I'll do that," replied Peddler Hinman, judging from the address on the letter, that was his name. "I don't like to be made a fool of by any man - especially when I need money as badly as any other man on my route."

Dick took a sweeping glance at the peddler's shabby attire. While, of course, the size of a man's bank account cannot be judged from his wardrobe, Mr. Hinman had the appearance of needing money as much as he declared. The horse, too, looked as though a generous feed of oats would do him good.

"And to think of all the things I know about Squire Stark, too," murmured Mr. Hinman, apparently speaking to himself and not realizing that his words carried to the boys' ears. "If he had a little more judgment, Silas Stark would treat me with more fairness."

"I'm very sorry if I seemed too much amused," Tom apologized earnestly, "but that letter, apart from its meaning to you, really is funny."

"I - -I suppose so," assented Reuben Hinman sighing, and the far-away look returning to his eyes. "But I - I need the money!"

"And both of us hope that you will get it, sir, the whole of your half," said Dick Prescott heartily.

"Anyway, I'm much obliged to both of you boys," said the peddler. "Giddap, Prince!"

Somehow, both boys thought that Reuben Hinman drooped more on the seat of his wagon than before. He drove off slowly, evidently doing a lot of hard thinking.

"Poor old man!" muttered Tom sympathetically.

"He looks a bit slow-witted," Prescott suggested. "I'm afraid he has always been going through life wondering at the doings of others, and especially at the success of unprincipled men he has had to deal with."

"Do you know," remarked Reade, gazing after the bent, huddled little figure, "I've a notion that there has been a lot in that poor fellow's life that has been downright tragic."

Tragic? Without doubt! Moreover, though Dick could not guess it, he and his friends were soon to be mixed up in the tragic side of Peddler Hinman's life.

H. Irving Hancock

CHAPTER IV

PEDDLER HINMAN'S NEXT APPEARANCE

Camp was made at half-past four that afternoon, nineteen miles having been covered. The tent was pitched in a bit of woods, not far from the road, permission from the owner having been secured.

Dave had asked the owner if they might picket the horse out to graze, but Dick had instantly objected.

"We don't want to feed our hired horse on green grass if we're going to work him hard."

"That's right," agreed the farmer, so twenty cents' worth of hay was purchased, to be added to the feed of oats.

"It's some fun to travel this way when we know we have money enough to pay our way like men," Tom Reade remarked exultingly.

For Dick & Co. were well supplied with funds. As told in the preceding volume in this series, they had, during July, realized enough from the sale of black bass and brook trout to enable them to have a thoroughly good time during this present month of August.

"Oh, Hazy!" called Reade, when it became time to think of supper.

"Here," reported Harry, rising from a cot in the tent and coming outside.

"It's time for you and Dan to rustle the firewood and bring in more water," Reade went on.

"All right," agreed Hazelton. "Where's Dan?"

Where, indeed, was Dalzell? That soon became a problem for all five of the other boys. Danny Grin was nowhere in sight.

"Dan! Oh, Dan!" Dave shouted.

"Where is that grinning monkey of a football player?" demanded Tom in disgust. "Did any of you fellows see him go away from camp?"

It turned out that none of them had.

"It isn't like Dalzell to run away from his share of the work, either," added Greg Holmes.

"If he won't stay and do his share toward getting supper, then he ought to be passed up at table," grumbled Darrin.

"Before we pass sentence," proposed Dick, "won't it be better to wait and find out whether he's guilty of shirking this time?"

"I suppose it would be better," Darrin admitted.

So the boys continued their preparations.

"What shall we have for the main thing to eat to-night?" Dick inquired, after supper preparations were well under way.

"Canned corned beef?" suggested Greg.

"That would be about as good as anything," Tom nodded. "It means two salted meats in one day, but this country is well supplied with water."

"We can't ask Danny Grin's preference this evening," Dick laughed. "I wonder what Dan would like, anyway?"

"Who's taking my name in vain?" demanded a laughing voice, as Dalzell appeared between the trees.

"Oh, you -"

"Shirk!" Reade had been about to add, when Danny held up a fat string of fish. These were horned-pouts, sometimes called "bull-heads."

"How many?" asked Dick promptly.

"Nineteen - one for every mile we made in getting close to the creek," Dan rejoined.

"Great!" cried Greg. "We haven't had any fish, either, since we returned from our trip to the second lake."

"How do you cook bull-heads?" Dave wondered aloud.

"With the aid of fire," Hazy informed him with an air

of superior knowledge.

"But I mean - I mean - " uttered Darry disgustedly, "how do you prepare bull-heads for cooking?"

"First of all, you clean 'em, as in the case of any other fish," proclaimed Tom Reade. "I defy any fellow to dispute me on that point."

"And then you wet the bull-head and roll him in corn meal, next dropping him into the pan and frying him to a fine brown," Dick supplemented.

"But we haven't any corn meal," objected Hazy.

"Yes, we have," Prescott corrected. "I saw to that last night. You fellows jump in and clean these fish, fast, while I get out the corn meal and put a pan on the fire."

These boys knew much more about cooking than falls to most boys in their teens. Frequent camping since their good old days in Central Grammar School had made them able to cook like veteran woodsmen.

Within two minutes, fat was sputtering in a hot pan, and Dick was shaking corn meal onto a plate.

"Bring 'em up!" he ordered. "We'll start this thing going."

Twenty minutes later, using two pans, all the bull-heads had been cooked, and now lay on platters in the oven of the stove.

"Three apiece, and one left over," Greg discovered. "Who gets the odd one?"

"Shame on you!" muttered Reade. "The horse gets the odd one, of course."

"A horse won't eat fish," Holmes retorted.

"Didn't you ever see a horse eat fish?" Tom challenged.

"I never did."

"Well, I don't know that I ever did, either," Reade admitted. "So we'll give the odd one to Danny Grin."

"Maybe we'll be glad to," laughed Dave. "I'm not sure that all these bull-heads were alive when Dalzell picked them up."

"Huh!" snorted Dan.

Nothing spoiled their appetite for the fish, however, which were cooked to a turn and of fine flavor. Tom Reade, however, got the odd fish as being the only one whose appetite was large enough to permit of the feat of adding it to three other fish.

"And now, what are we going to do?" asked Dave, after the meal was finished and the dishes had been washed.

"Who has sore feet?" called Dick.

Not one of the six boys would plead guilty to that charge.

"Then we won't have to heat water," Dick announced. "Each fellow can bathe his feet in cold water before turning in. But, when one's feet ache, or are blistered, then a wash in piping hot water is the thing to take out the ache."

By nine o'clock all hands began to feel somewhat drowsy, for the day had been warm, and, at last, these youngsters were willing to admit that their road work had been as strenuous as they needed.

"But to-morrow we'll do twenty-five miles," Dave insisted.

"My opinion is that we'll do well if we make twenty miles to-morrow," Dick rejoined.

"But what are we going to do now?" yawned Hazy, as they sat about under the light of two lanterns.

"Go to bed," declared Greg.

"Hooray! That's the ticket that I vote," announced Hazy.

"I was just thinking of that mean lawyer we heard about to-day," Reade remarked.

"I was thinking of the same matter, but more about the poor old peddler," Dick stated. "That poor old fellow! I'll wager he has had a hard time all through life, and that he's still wondering why it all had to happen. How old would you say Mr. Hinman is, Tom?"

"He'll never have a seventieth birthday again," replied Reade thoughtfully. "My! A man at that age ought not to have to bother with working. It's pitiful. It's a shame!"

"Maybe he finds his only happiness in work," Darrin suggested. "I have known old people like that."

By this time Dan had taken one of the lanterns into the tent, and was undressing. Dave soon followed, then Greg and Hazelton.

"Do you want to take a little walk down to the road, where we can get a better look at the sky?" Dick proposed to Reade. "We ought to take a squint at the weather."

"That will suit me," Tom nodded, so away they strolled toward the road.

"If you fellows stay away from camp long, don't you be mean enough to talk, or make any other noise when you get back to the tent," Darrin called after them.

Down by the road there was a breeze blowing, and it was cooler.

"I'd like to bring my cot down this way," Tom suggested.

"There's no law against it," Dick smiled. "The owner's permission extended in a general way to all the land right around here."

"Will you bring your cot, too?" Tom asked.

"Certainly."

So, before any of the other fellows were asleep, Dick and Tom reentered the tent to get their folding cots and bedding.

"Cooler down by the road, is it?" asked Darrin wistfully. "Then I'm sorry you didn't find it out before I undressed."

"We'll sleep in our clothes," Dick replied. "Come along, Tom, and give the infant class a chance to get to sleep."

After lying, fully dressed on their cots, which they placed within ten feet of the road, Dick and Tom found themselves so wide awake that they lay chatting for some moments.

At last Reade mumbled his answers; next his unmistakably deep breathing indicated that he was asleep. Prescott thereupon turned over on his side and dozed off.

It was shortly after their first few moments of sleep had passed that a noise in the road close by awoke both boys.

Dick sat up leaning on one elbow, listening. Someone was coming toward them.

As the stranger came closer, Dick, his eyes seeing well in the dark, made out the unmistakable form of Reuben Hinman, the peddler.

"What's he doing out here at this hour of the night, and on foot?" wondered Dick Prescott half aloud.

"Eh? What?" asked Reade in a low, drowsy voice, as he opened his eyes.

"It's Mr. Hinman, the peddler," Prescott whispered to

his chum. "But I wonder what's wrong with him?"

"I wonder, too," Reade assented. "One thing is certain; something has happened to him."

For Reuben Hinman half-lurched, half-staggered along, yet his gait did not suggest intoxication. He moved, rather, as one who is dazed with trouble.

The old man was sobbing, too, with a sound that was pitiful to hear; as though some great grief were clutching at his heart.

CHAPTER V

DAVE DOES SOME GOOD WORK

"Good evening, Mr. Hinman!" called Dick softly.

The old man started, affrighted.

"Who - -who calls?" he quavered.

"One of the boys you talked with, this noon."

"Where are you?"

"Here," answered Dick, throwing his blanket aside, rising and stepping toward the old man, who, more bent than ever, was shaking as though from fright. "Don't be afraid of us, sir. Can we help you in anything?"

"I am afraid not," replied the peddler, then leaned against a tree-trunk, staring, as he tried to stifle his sobs.

"What has happened, sir?" asked Tom Reade, also stepping forward.

"I've been robbed!" replied the old man, in a broken voice.

H. Irving Hancock

"Robbed?" repeated Dick. "Do you mean that some villains have stolen the goods from your wagon?"

"No, no!" replied the old man, with sudden, unlooked for vehemence. "I've been robbed, I tell you - my money stolen!"

"Money?" asked Tom in surprise. "How much was taken from you?"

"Four hundred and eighteen dollars," replied the old man, with a lack of reserve that testified to his confidence in these unknown but respectful and sympathetic high school boys.

"All that money?" cried Dick. "How did you ever come to have so much about you?"

"I owe some bills for goods, over at Hillsboro," replied Reuben Hinman, "and this trip was to take me toward Hillsboro. But now -"

He broke off, the strange, rending sobbing returning.

"Perhaps we can help you, bad as the case looks," Tom suggested. "Try to tell us all about it, sir."

"Where did you have the money?" inquired Dick.

"In a wallet, in this inside coat pocket," replied the peddler, holding his frayed coat open at the right side.

"You carried your wallet as conspicuously as that when traveling over lonely country roads?" cried Prescott in amazement.

"I had a lot of letters and papers in front of the wallet, so that no one would suspect that I had the wallet or the money," explained Reuben Hinman.

"I don't see any papers there now," Tom interposed.

"They're gone," replied Mr. Hinman. "Probably the thief thought the papers valuable, also, but they weren't. -"

"You were robbed - when?" asked Dick.

"When I was sleeping."

"At some farm house?" Reade inquired.

"No; I slept on a pile of old rags that I had taken in trade."

"In the wagon? -" from Prescott.

"Yes."

"But why did you sleep in the wagon? And where did you have the wagon?" Dick pressed.

"The wagon was off the road, two miles below here," the peddler explained brokenly. "It would cost me fifty cents for a bed at a farm house, so, when the night is fine, I sleep outdoors on the wagon and save the money. It's cheaper with the horse, too, as I have to pay only for his feed."

"But the money?" Tom pressed the old man. Reuben Hinman groaned, but did not take to sobbing again.

"I woke up to-night, and found it gone," he answered.

"Did you feel or hear anyone prowling about, or searching your clothing?"

"No; if I had discovered anyone robbing me," shivered the peddler, "I would have caught and held on to him. I have strong hands. I have strong hands. Do you see?"

Holding up his wiry, claw-like hands, the old peddler worked the fingers convulsively.

"Then how do you know you were robbed, Mr. Hinman?" Dick insisted.

"Because the money is gone," replied the old man simply.

"You searched the rags, and the surrounding parts of your wagon?" Reade asked.

"Young man, you may be sure that I did."

"And where were you going when we stopped you?"

"For help."

"Whose help?" Dick inquired.

"I don't know," replied the old man blankly. "Perhaps to a lawyer."

"Lawyers don't recover stolen property," rejoined Reade.

"Perhaps not," assented the peddler. "The people

whom you should see are the local officers," Dick assured the old man. "Probably they couldn't recover your money, though, since you have no idea who robbed you."

Reuben Hinman groaned helplessly. It was plain to the two high school boys that the peddler had started out, thus, in the middle of the night simply because his misery was too great to permit of inaction on his part.

"I wish we could help you," Prescott went on earnestly.

"Why can't you?" eagerly demanded the peddler, as one who clutches at the frailest straw.

"Call Dave, Tom. Try not to wake the others," murmured Dick. Then, while Reade was gone, Prescott asked:

"Mr. Hinman, why on earth didn't you keep your money in a bank, and then pay by check?"

"No, no, no! No banks for me!" cried the old man tremulously.

"Are you afraid to trust banks with your money?" demanded Dick incredulously.

"No, no! It isn't that," protested the peddler confusedly. "The banks are all right, and honest men run them. But -"

Whatever was in his mind he checked himself. It was as though he had been on the verge of uttering words that must not be spoken.

Dick Prescott found himself obliged to turn his eyes away. It was altogether too pitiful, the look in old Reuben Hinman's shriveled face. In his misery the small, stooped peddler looked still smaller and more bent.

Tom soon came along, carrying a lantern and followed by Dave, the latter yawning every step of the way.

"Now, which way are we going to look first?" Reade inquired.

"I've been thinking that over," Dick replied. "It seems to me that the sanest course will be to start right at the scene of the robbery. From there we may get a clue that we can follow somewhere."

"Yes, that's as good a course as any," nodded Darrin, who had received some of the particulars of the affair from Reade.

So the three high school boys started off down the road together, old Reuben Hinman trudging tirelessly along with them, acting like a man in a trance.

At last they came to the old, red wagon. The tethered horse, disturbed, rose to its feet.

"Now, the rest of you keep away," requested young Prescott, "until I've had time to look all around the wagon with the lantern. I want to see if I can discover any footprints that will help."

For a considerable radius around the wagon the high school athlete scanned the ground. He could find no footprints, other than those of Reuben Hinman, and the fresher ones made by himself.

"Nothing doing in the footprint line, boys," Dick called at last. "Now, come along and we'll search the wagon."

"Let me have the first chance," begged Dave, taking the lantern.

Reuben Hinman showed where he had slept on the pile of rags, but this was hardly necessary, the impression made by his slight body being still visible.

Dave began to rummage. At last he got down into the body of the wagon. With the rays of the lantern thus concealed, the other three stood in darkness.

"Hooray!" gasped Dave at last. Then rising, leaning over the side of the wagon, he called:

"Mr. Hinman, I've found a wallet, with a lot of greenbacks inside. How much I don't know. Please count it and see if all the money is there intact."

With an inarticulate cry the old peddler seized the wallet that was handed down to him. He shook like a leaf as Tom held the lantern for him to count the money. Now that the strain was over, Mr. Hinman's legs became suddenly too weak to support him. He sank to the ground, Tom squatting close so that the lantern's rays would fall where they would be most useful. Thus the old peddler counted his money with trembling fingers.

"Where did you find the wallet?" young Prescott asked Darrin.

H. Irving Hancock

"Up against the side of the wagon, under a partly tilted, upsidedown feed-pail," Dave answered. "I can understand why Mr. Hinman didn't find it. He was too much upset - too nervous, and it certainly didn't look like a likely place."

"It must have fallen out of his pocket as he slept," Prescott guessed correctly. "Did you find any papers down there on the floor of the wagon?"

"Yes; some sort of paper stuff," nodded Dave. "I took it for rubbish."

"The money is all here!" cried the old peddler, in a frenzy of joy. "Oh, how can I thank you young men? You don't know what your blessed help means for me!"

"Was it all the money you had?" Dick asked feelingly.

"Yes; all except for few loose dollars that I have in a little sack in my trousers pocket," replied Mr. Hinman.

"Then it was all you had in the world, outside of your peddling stock and your horse and cart?" Prescott continued.

"All except a little house and barn that I own, and the small piece of ground they stand on," said the peddler. "If I had not found my money I would have been obliged to mortgage my little home to a bank - and then I am afraid I could not have repaid the bank, and my home would be taken from me."

"But you would have found the money in the wagon some day soon," suggested Dick.

"Perhaps," replied the peddler. "Who knows? Perhaps someone else would have rummaged the wagon and found it before I did. Oh! It might have been taken a little while ago, even when I was toiling down the road, or talking with you boys at your camp!" he added, with a sudden wave of fright over the thought.

"One thing is certain, anyhow, Mr. Hinman," Dick concluded. "Someone may have overheard you talking with us about this money. You will hardly be safe here. I urge you to come to our camp, and there spend the night with boys who know how to take care of themselves, and who can look after you at need. You will not be attacked in our camp."

Reuben Hinman eagerly agreeing, Dave harnessed the bony horse into the wagon. After a while the red wagon rested within the confines of the camp of Dick & Co.

In the bright light of the morning, Harry Hazelton was the first to be astir. He saw Prescott asleep on the floor of the tent, rolled up in a blanket, while another blanket rested on Dick's cot, brought back to the tent, as though some stranger had slept there.

Outside, attached to the seat of their camp wagon, Hazy found a note that mystified him a good deal at first. It read:

"The sun is now well up. I shall go at once to Hillsboro, and then my great worry will be over. Boys, you will ever be remembered in the prayers of R.H."

"Now, that's mighty nice of R.H., whoever he is," smiled Harry Hazelton, not immediately connecting the initials with the name of the little, old peddler.

Nor was it until Prescott and Reade were astir that Harry was fully enlightened as to the meaning of the words scrawled in pencil on the sheet of paper.

"You boys call me Hazy, and I must look and act the part," laughed Hazelton shamefacedly, "when we can have such an invasion of the camp, and such an early get-away with a loaded wagon, and all without my stirring."

Reuben Hinman was on his way, and, all unknown to himself nearer the hour when he would meet the high, school boys under vastly more exciting circumstances.

CHAPTER VI

THE NO-BREAKFAST PLAN

"Let's get the tent down, fellows," Dick called. "Greg is loading the bedding on to the wagon now."

"Haven't, you forgotten something?" Danny Grin asked.

"What?" challenged Dick smilingly.

"Well, a little thing like breakfast, for instance?"

"We don't get that until after we've had our swim," Prescott rejoined cheerily.

"I suppose that's all right," observed Tom, his jaw dropping. "Still, in that case, Mr. Trainer, why didn't you camp nearer to a stream?"

"The nearest stream fit for swimming is two miles from here," Dick replied. "At least, that's what I judge from the map."

"There's the creek the bull-heads came from," suggested Hazelton hopefully. "That's close at hand."

"I know it is," Dick replied, "but I've had a look at it.

　　　　　　H. Irving Hancock

That creek is both shallow and muddy. No sort of place for swimming."

One thing these Gridley High School boys had learned in the football squad, and that was discipline. So, though there were some gloomy looks, all remembered that Dick had been chosen trainer during the hike, and that his word, in training matters, was to be their law. So the tent came down, in pretty nearly record time, and was loaded on the wagon. The horse was harnessed, also without breakfast, and the party started down the road with Harry Hazelton holding the reins.

"I hope it's a short two miles," growled Reade to Darrin.

"Humph! A fine Indian you'd make, Tom!" jibed Dave. "An Indian is trained in being hungry. It's a part of the work that he has to undergo before he is allowed to be one of the men of the tribe."

"That's just the trouble with me," Tom admitted. "I've never been trained to be an Indian, and I am inclined to think that it requires training, and a lot of it."

Outwardly Tom didn't "grump" any, but he made a resolve that, hereafter, his voice would be strong for halting right on the bank of a swimming place.

"Can't we hit up the pace a bit?" asked Tom.

"Yes," nodded Dick. "All who want to travel fast can hike right ahead. Just keep on the main road."

Tom, Greg and Dan immediately forged ahead, taking long, rapid steps.

"But don't go in the water until we come up," Dick called after them. "Remember, the morning is hot, and you'll be too overheated to go in at once."

"Eh?" muttered Tom, with a sidelong look at his two fast-time companions. "Humph!"

Then they fell back with the wagon again.

"There doesn't seem to be any way to beat the clock to breakfast," observed Dan, after he had walked several rods down the road.

"I've talked with old soldiers," Dick went on, "who have told me all sorts of tales of war time, about the commissary train not catching up with the fighting line for four days at a stretch. Yet here you fellows feel almost ill if you have to put off breakfast half an hour. What kind of men would you boys make if it came to the stern part of life?"

"If going without breakfast is part of the making of a man," said Danny Grin solemnly, "then I'd rather be a child some more."

"You always will be a child," Dave observed dryly. "Birthdays won't make any great difference in your real age, Danny boy."

"After that kind of a roast," grinned Reade, "I believe I'll take a reef in a few of the bitter things I was about to say."

Dick laughed pleasantly. Somehow, with the walk, all soon began to feel better. That first fainting, yearning desire for food was beginning to pass.

"Do you know what the greatest trouble is with the American people?" asked Dick, after they had covered a mile.

"I don't," Tom admitted. "Do you, Dick?"

"I've been forming an idea," Prescott went on. "Our fault, if I can gather it rightly from what I've been reading, is that we Americans are inclined to be too babyish."

"Tell that to the countries we've been at war with in the past," jeered Tom Reade.

"Oh, I guess it's a different breed of Americans that we send to the front in war time," Prescott continued. "But, take you fellows; some of you have been almost kicking because breakfast is put off a bit. Most Americans are like that. Yet, it isn't because we have such healthy stomachs, either, for foreigners know us as a race of dyspeptics. Take a bit of cold weather in winter - really cold, biting weather and just notice how Americans kick and worry about it. Take any time when we have a succession of rainy days, and notice how Americans growl over the continued wet. Whatever happens that is in the least disagreeable, see what a row we Americans raise about it."

"I imagine it's a nervous vent for the race," advanced Dave Darrin.

"But why must Americans have a nervous vent?" Dick inquired. "In other words, what business have we with diseased nerves! Don't you imagine that all our kicking, many times every day of our lives, makes the need of nervous vent more and more pronounced?"

"Oh, I don't know about that," argued Tom. "I hate to hear any fellow talk disparagingly about his own country or its people. It doesn't sound just right. In war time, or during any great national disaster or calamity, the Americans who do things always seem to rise to the occasion. We're a truly great people, all right. But I don't make that claim because I consider myself ever likely to be one of the great ones."

"Why are we a great people?" pursued Prescott.

"We are the richest nation in the world," argued Reade. "That must show that we are people capable of making great successes."

"Is our greatness due to ourselves, or to the fact that the United States embraces the greatest natural resources in the world?" demanded Dick Prescott.

"It's partly due to the people, and partly due to the resources of the country," Dave contended.

Dick kept them arguing. Harry Hazelton, as driver, remained silent, but the others argued against Dick, trying to overthrow all his disparaging utterances against the American people.

Finally Reade grew warm, indeed.

"Cut it out, Dick - do!" he urged. "This doesn't really sound like you. I hate to hear a fellow go on running down his own countrymen. I tell you, it isn't patriotic."

"But just stop to consider this point," Prescott urged, and started on a new, cynical line of argument.

"I still contend that we're the greatest people on earth," Reade insisted almost angrily. "We ought to be, anyway, for Americans don't come of any one line of stock. We're descended from pioneers - the pick and cream of all the peoples of Europe."

But Dick kept up his line of discussion until they came to the river for which he had headed them. They followed the winding stream into the woods where the trees partially hid them from the observation of passers-by on the road, From this point they could easily keep a watch on the wagon while in the water.

"Now, let's sit down and cool off for five minutes," proposed Dick, as he filled the feed bag for the horse. "After that we'll be ready for a swim."

"But, with regard to what you were saying about frayed American nerves, poor stomachs and all-around babyishness -" Tom began all over again.

"Stop it!" laughed Dick. "We don't need that line of talk any longer."

"Then why did you start it?" asked Dave.

"We've covered the two miles that you all thought such a hardship," chuckled Prescott.

"Then you -" began Reade, opening his eyes wider as a dawning light came into them. "Come on, Dave! Catch him! The water's handy!"

But Dick, with a light laugh, bounded away, shinned up a tree, and, sitting in a crotch, swung his feet toward the faces of Tom, Dave and Harry as they tried to get him and drag him down.

"You've got a strategic position, just now," growled Reade. "But just you wait until we catch you down on the ground again!"

"You fellows must feel pretty well sold," Greg taunted them. "I kept out of the row, for I saw, at the outset, that Dick was going to start something for the sole purpose of keeping us arguing until we forgot all about our breakfasts."

"That's just like Dick Prescott!" uttered Tom ruefully. "We never get to know him so well that he can't start us all on a new tack and have more fun with us."

"Well, you forgot your supposed starvation, didn't you?" chuckled Dick from his tree.

Two or three minutes later he swung down from the tree to the ground, rapidly removing his clothing and donning swimming trunks. He was not molested; the other five were too busy preparing for the bath.

"The water's great to-day!" shouted Dick, rising and "blowing" after a shallow dive from a tree trunk at the shore.

In a moment they were all in the water.

"Come on! Follow your leader!" shouted Tom Reade, striking out lustily upstream.

"Come back and give us a handicap!" roared Dave. "How do you expect us to catch you when you get the lead over us with your long legs and arms?"

H. Irving Hancock

But Tom dived under water, swimming there. The others followed suit, each remaining under as long as possible, for, in this "stunt," there was no way of knowing when the leader came up. Tom remained under less than fifteen seconds. Then, showing his head, and with rapid overhand strokes he made for the nearer bank, slipping ashore and hiding behind some bushes.

It was Hazy who had to come up first after Tom.

"Whew! Tom must have met someone he knows on the bottom," called Harry, as Greg's head rose above the surface.

Dave came up next, then Dick, and then Dan.

"Tom ought to be a fish!" uttered Darrin admiringly. "I stayed under water as long as I could."

Yet after going a few yards further up stream Dick Prescott turned, gazing anxiously down stream.

"Fellows," he suggested, "something must have happened to old Tom."

"Or else he's playing a joke on us," hinted Danny Grin, suspiciously.

"It's some joke to remain under water four times as long as the average swimmer can do it," retorted Prescott.

"But Tom may not be under water," spoke up Greg.

"He didn't have time to get anywhere else," Dave declared.

"It may be a joke, but I don't want to take any chances," Dick said earnestly. "Let's go down stream. Spread out, and every now and then bob under and take as near a look at the bottom as you can."

"It doesn't look right," Dave admitted as they all started back.

Several times they went under water, the best swimmers among them getting close to bottom. So they continued on down the stream for some distance.

"Now, all together. Go under water all at the same time," ordered Dick.

Below the surface of the river they went. One after another their heads presently appeared above the surface once more.

"Have you fellows lost anything?" quizzed Reade, suddenly appearing on the bank.

"That's what I call a mean trick on us!" cried Dave, flushing slightly.

"You fellows were in for a swim, weren't you?" Reade drawled. "You have been having it."

With that he took to the water himself. There was something so jovial and harmless about Reade that, despite their recent anxiety concerning him, they made no effort to duck him.

"The water is fine this morning," called Tom presently, as they all swam about.

"Then why didn't you stay in?" demanded Darry rather cuttingly.

"Say, I'm beginning to feel glad that I waited breakfast for the swim," Reade announced.

"Stick to the truth!" mocked Dick.

"But I really am beginning to feel that a little exercise is the best course before breakfast," Tom declared.

"The next thing we hear," scoffed Hazy, "you'll be telling us that you really don't want any breakfast."

"I'll tell you fellows what I'll do," Tom called. "I'll agree to put off eating until noon if you'll all stick to the idea."

But that suggestion did not prove popular.

"I mean it," Reade insisted. "I hardly care, now, whether I eat any breakfast or not."

"What's that noise below? Come on!" called Prescott, landing and running along the bank. Tom was close behind him, the others following.

In their search for Tom they had gotten farther away from the wagon than they realized. During their brief absence from the spot two tramps had come upon the camp wagon and the piles of discarded clothing. It was plain that the wagon contained all that was needed for several meals - -and the tramps were hungry.

Yet the only safe way to enjoy that food would be to partake of it at a safe distance from the rightful owners.

For that reason, after a few whispered words, the tramps hastily gathered up all the clothing of the high school swimmers, dumping it in the wagon. Then they mounted to the seat.

Just as Dick Prescott and his chums broke from cover they beheld the tramps in the act of driving from the woods out on the road.

Once in the road the tramps urged the horse to a gallop. It was out of the question for the boys, clad as they were in only swimming trunks to pursue the thieves.

"I - I - take back all I said about not wanting any breakfast!" gasped Tom Reade, turning to his dismayed chums.

H. Irving Hancock

CHAPTER VII

MAKING THE TRAMPS SQUIRM

"You come back here!" screamed Danny Grin desperately.

"Haven't time now," called one of the tramps jeeringly, while his companion laid the whip over the startled horse.

With such a start as the tramps had they might be able to drive a mile ere the running boys could overtake them.

Besides, both law and custom forbade six boys clad only in bathing trunks from running along the highway.

"You'll find the wagon a few miles from here!" jeered the tramp who held the reins. "We'll leave it when we're through with it. We -"

But further words could not be heard for the wagon had vanished from view at a turn in the road between the trees.

"We're in a bad pickle, now!" gasped Tom Reade.

But Dick, studying the lay of the land with swift glances, saw just one chance. If the tramps turned the horse in the right direction on gaining the highway -

Dick broke off his thoughts there.

"Tom, you and Dave pursue a little way and travel like lightning," ordered young Prescott. "The rest of you pick up stones! Fast! Come along now."

On reaching the highway the driver was forced to make a little turn in order to cross the bridge, in case he decided to travel in the direction that the boys had been going. So Dick dashed ahead, hoping to profit by the one chance he saw.

Just as luck would have it, the tramps turned in the right direction. The horse, galloping fast under the lash, struck his forefeet on the bridge.

Whack! clatter! plug! Four high school boys, all of them baseball players and proud of their straight throwing, sent a small shower of rocks whizzing through the air.

These struck the bridge planks well ahead of the horse.

"Stop - or the next ones will hit you!" shouted young Prescott.

Just by way of suggestion he threw one stone that flew by within a foot of the nearer tramp's head. Holmes duplicated the throw.

"Stop that!" yelled one of the tramps, but he brought the horse to a standstill.

H. Irving Hancock

"Don't you throw any more stones!" yelled the tramp, as he saw the four ball players poised ready for more work in that line.

"Then hold the horse where he is until we come and take him," ordered Dick.

"We won't, and don't you throw any more stones," ordered the tramp. "Jerry, turn your pistol loose on the young cubs if they throw another stone. Giddap!"

"That's a bluff. You haven't any pistol," Dick called to the tramps coolly. "Just start that horse, and we'll knock both your heads off with stones. We know how to throw 'em."

Splash! Greg Holmes had taken to the narrow river. Now he was striking out lustily for the other side. In case the horse was started Holmes would be there, with a handful of stones with which to bombard the fugitives in passing.

"You fellers quit throwing stones, or you're going to get hurt!"

But the pause had accomplished the very thing for which Dick had waited.

"Throw another stone," repeated the tramp, "and you'll get -"

"Oh, tell it to the Senate!" broke in Tom Reade, climbing into the wagon and seizing the speaker. Dave, who had crept up with him, had gripped the other tramp by the collar.

Both tramps were thrown from the seat. Ere they could recover from their astonishment, Reade and Darrin had leaped down upon their tormentors.

"In with them!" ordered Dick.

Two splashes, occurring almost in the same second, testified to the tackling skill that Reade and Darrin had acquired on the gridiron.

Dick and his friends stood by to rescue the tramps, in case either of them could not swim.

Both could, however, and struck out for the shore, abusing the boys roundly as they swam.

Dave had seized the horse's bridle, and was now turning the animal about. Tom walked on the other side of the wagon.

"Look out, Greg!" called Dick suddenly, as the tramps, gaining the opposite shore, made a sudden rush at Holmes, who stood alone.

"I can take care of myself!" chuckled Greg gleefully, as dodging backward, he poised his right hand to throw a stone. "Look out, friends, unless you want to get hurt!"

Both tramps halted in a good deal of uncertainty. They wanted to thrash this high school boy, but they didn't like the risk of having their heads hurt by flying stones.

Two splashes on the other side of the river heralded the fact that Dan and Harry had started to Greg's aid. The instant they saw this, both men turned away from

Greg, making a dash for the highway.

Laughing, young Holmes followed them up with all the missiles he had left. Not one dropped further than three feet from the flying heels of the fugitives, yet not one struck either of the tramps or was meant to do so.

"Come across, you three fellows," laughed young Prescott, when the enemy had vanished in flight. You've all earned your breakfast now, and you shall have it."

"As for me," spoke Tom from the wagon, as he drove into the forest path, "I'm strong for putting on my clothes before I sit down to dally with food."

Reade did not wait until he had driven the wagon where he and his friends could dress away from the view of people on the road.

"The cast-iron cheek of those scoundrels!" vented Dave Darrin indignantly.

"I rather think we are their debtors," smiled Dick quietly, as he drew his shirt over his head.

"You do!" demanded Darry incredulously.

"Yes; just think of all the zest they've put into our morning, and they didn't harm us, either."

"But just think of what it would have been like if we hadn't stopped 'em!" gasped Danny Grin solemnly. "We couldn't have chased 'em. It wouldn't have been decent for us to go along the roa d, makingfour miles to every five covered by the horse. No, sir! We'd have had to remain hidden in the forest until we could signal some farmer to send to our folks for clothes to put on. Wouldn't it have been great, staying in the woods two or three days, with nothing to eat, waiting for the proper clothing to enable us to go out into the world again!"

"It was a mean trick!" cried Darry hotly; and then he began to laugh as the ridiculous features of the situation appealed to him.

"But nothing serious happened," laughed Dick, "so we owe that pair of tramps for a pleasant touch to the morning's sport."

"I wonder how many years since either of them has had a bath, until this morning," grinned Reade, as he began to lace his shoes.

As Reade was dressed first, Dick called to him: "Take the horse out of the shafts, Tom, and let him feed in comfort."

"You may," laughed Reade. "As for me, I've flirted with my breakfast so long this morning, and have taken so many chances of not having any, that now I'm going to make sure of that first of all."

So Dick himself attended to the horse. Dan was already gathering firewood, which Dave piled into the stove in the wagon.

Soon water was boiling, coffee was being ground, tins opened, and a general air of comfort and good fellowship prevailed in that forest.

"We'll have to give you the palm for being a good trainer, Dick," declared Tom, taking a bite out of a sandwich and following it with a sip of coffee, "but you have one short-coming. You're no fortune teller. So, as you can't foretell the future, I vote that, after this, we breakfast in the morning and swim later in the day. It would affect my heart in time, if we had to battle every morning for our breakfast in this fashion."

"I can't get over the impudence of those tramps," muttered Darry, as he set his coffee cup down. "They couldn't hope to get away with the horse and wagon and sell them in these days of the rural telephone. They couldn't use our clothing for themselves. And yet they stole all we had in order to get hold of our food. At that, they didn't care what became of us, or how long we had to travel about in these woods without food or clothing."

"The tramps must be optimists," laughed Prescott. "Probably they had an abiding faith that all would turn out well with us, and so proposed to help themselves to what they needed."

"I wonder whether they'll fool with our outfit again," pondered Tom grimly, "if they come across it in our absence."

"I don't know," said Dick gravely. "As you've already reminded me, I am no foreteller of the future."

CHAPTER VIII

WHEN THE PEDDLER WAS "FRISKED"

It was a hot and dusty road that lay before them when they again took up their march that day.

Yet Dick Prescott insisted that, despite the late start, they must count upon covering twenty miles for that second day.

At night they halted on the edge of woods so far from the nearest farm house that Prescott did not consider it necessary to hunt up the owner and ask permission.

"Now, we'll have to see if we can find water here," Dick proposed. "Let's scatter, and the fellow who finds drinkable water must let out a yell to inform the others."

"I'll save you some trouble," Reade offered. "You fellows needn't hunt water at all. Give me the buckets and I'll go and get it."

"Have you been in this part of the country before?" asked Dick.

"No; and I don't need to have been here before in order to know that this ground is full of water," replied

H. Irving Hancock

Reade, who was full of practical knowledge of that sort. "If I were a civil engineer, out with a field party, I'd mark this section 'water' on the map. Look at the ground here under the trees. It's as moist as can be."

Tom departed, but barely two minutes had elapsed when he was back with two pailfuls of water as clear as crystal.

"It's nearly as cold as ice water," Tom announced. "There's a bully big spring just a few steps back in the woods."

"Then I'm going to use some of this to wash up," Darrin declared. "I'll go with you on the next trip, Tom, and help carry the water."

"You'd better wait until we get the tent up before we wash," suggested Prescott. "Then you'll need it more."

Quick work was made of the encamping. Dan and Greg, from the wagon, passed down the tent itself, the floor boards and joists, the cots and bedding and some of the food supplies.

Then all hands quickly put up the tent. Reade and Hazelton had the flooring down in a jiffy. Dan and Greg put up the cots, while Dick and Dave set up the folding camp table and started the fire in the stove with a bundle of fagots brought in by Hazelton.

"Now, get busy with the wash-up," Dick called.

Within thirty minutes after halting, supper was on the table.

"How far from a swimming place this time?" Tom asked.

"Three miles, if I've studied the map right," replied Prescott, taking the road map from his pocket and passing it over.

"To-morrow," said Dave, "some of us will swim in plain sight of the outfit all the time."

"Do you think you can hike three miles and swim before breakfast in the morning?" asked Dick.

"The way I feel now," said Tom, pushing his campstool back from the table, "I shan't need anything to eat to-morrow."

"You must feel ill, then," declared Danny Grin.

"No; I feel just filed up enough to last for two or three days," sighed Reade contentedly.

Harry and Greg were a bit footsore, but the other boys claimed to feel all right.

"Do any of you feel like taking an evening walk?" asked Dick with a smile.

"I do," Darrin declared promptly.

"Not I," replied Tom. "At least not so soon after supper."

"Shall we try the walk?" Dick asked Darrin.

"I'm ready," Dave agreed. "Come along, then." Though

it was dark, the two boys decided not to take a lantern with them.

"We don't need one on a public highway," said Dick as they plunged off down the dark road.

"How far shall we go?" Darrin asked.

"I think two miles away from camp and two miles back, ought to be far enough," Dick replied.

"If we feel like going farther, we can tackle it when the time comes," Darrin answered. "But how shall we judge the distance?"

"We'll walk briskly for thirty-five to thirty-eight minutes," Prescott suggested. "Then we'll turn back. While we're out we may get some idea of whether there's a swimming place nearer than three miles from camp."

Neither felt in the least footsore. Indeed, these two hardy high school boys thoroughly enjoyed their tramp in this cooler part of the twenty-four hours.

"I wish we could live outdoors all the time," murmured Darrin, as he filled his lungs with the fine night air.

"A lot of folks have felt that way," smiled Dick. "The idea is all right, too, only the work of the civilized world couldn't be carried on by a lot of tramps without homes or places of business."

"I've heard, or read," Darry went on, "that a tramp, after one season on the road, is rarely ever reclaimed to useful work. I think I can understand something of the fascination of the life."

"I can't see any fascination about being a tramp," Prescott replied judicially. "First of all, he becomes a vagabond, who prefers idleness to work. Then, too, he becomes dirty, and I can't see any charm in a life that is divorced from baths. From mere idleness the tramp soon finds that petty thieving is an easy way to get along. If I were going to be a thief at all, I'd want to be an efficient one. No stealing of wash from a clothesline, or of pies from a housekeeper's pantry, when there are millions to be stolen in the business world."

"Now, you're laughing at me," uttered Dave.

"No; I'm not."

"But you wouldn't steal money if you had millions right under your hand where you could get away with the stuff," protested Darry.

"I wouldn't," Dick agreed promptly. "I wouldn't steal anything. Yet it's no worse, morally, to steal a million dollars from a great bank than it is to steal a suit of clothes from a house whose occupants are absent. All theft is theft. There are no degrees of theft. The small boy who would steal a nickel or a dime from his mother would steal a million dollars from a stranger if he had the chance and the nerve to commit the crime. All tramps, sooner or later, become petty thieves. Thieving goes with the life of idleness and vagabondage."

"I don't know about that," argued Dave. "A lot of men become tramps just through hard luck. I don't believe all of them steal, even small stuff."

H. Irving Hancock

"I believe they do, if they remain tramps," Dick insisted. "No man is safe who will deliberately go through life without earning his way. The man who starts with becoming idle ends with becoming vicious. This doesn't apply to tramps alone. Any day's newspaper will furnish you with stories of the vicious doings of the idle sons of rich men. Unless a man has an object in life, and works directly toward it all the time, he is in danger."

"I'd hate to believe that every ragged tramp I meet is a criminal," Dave muttered.

"He is, if he remains a tramp long enough," Dick declared with emphasis. "Take the tramps we met this morning. Look at all the trouble they were taking to rob us of food for a meal or two."

"There may have been an element of mischief in what they did," Dave hinted. "They may have done it just as a lark."

"They were thieves by instinct," Dick insisted. "They would have stolen anything that they could get away with safely. Hello! There's a light over there in the woods."

"Another camping party?" Dave wondered.

"Tramps, more likely. Suppose we speak low and advance with caution until we know where we are and whom we're likely to meet."

In silence the high school boys drew nearer. The light proved to come from a campfire that had been lighted some fifty feet from the road.

"Yes, you have!" insisted a harsh voice, as the boys drew nearer. "Don't try to fool with us. Turn over your money, or we'll make you wish you had!"

"Why, it's our tramps of this morning," whispered Dave.

"And look at that wagon - the peddler's!" Dick whispered in answer.

"Come, now, old man! Turn over your money, unless you want us to frisk you for it!" continued a voice.

"There are your honest tramps, Dave," Prescott whispered.

Then his eyes flashed, for, by the light of the campfire the lads saw the tramps seize frightened Reuben Hinman on either side and literally turn him upside down, the old man's head hitting the ground.

"Don't make any noise," whispered Prescott, "but we won't stand for that!"

"We surely won't!" Darry agreed with emphasis.

"Come on, now - soft-foot!"

As the tramps jostled Mr. Hinman, upside down and yelling with fright, a sack containing the peddler's money rolled from one of the peddler's trousers pockets.

"Shake him again! There'll be more than that coming!" jeered one of the tramps.

But just then they let go their hold of the old man, for Dick Prescott and Dave Darrin rushed in out of the darkness, dealing blows that sent the tramps swiftly to earth.

Yet the two high school boys were now doomed to pay the penalty of not having scouted a bit before rushing in.

For the two tramps were not the only ones of their kind at hand. Out of the shadows under the surrounding trees came a rush of feet, accompanied by hoarse yells.

Then, before they had had time fully to realize just what was happening, Prescott and Darrin found themselves suddenly in the midst of the worst fight they had ever seen in their lives.

"Beat 'em up!" yelled the man whom Dick had knocked down. "I know these young fellers! They put up a bad time for us this morning. Beat 'em up and make a good job of it, too."

There was no use whatever in contending with such odds. Yet Dick and Dave fought with all their might, only to be borne to the ground, where they received severe punishment.

CHAPTER IX

DICK IMITATES A TAME INDIAN

"Hello! hello!" yelled Tom Reade, pacing up and down the road with his lantern, holding his watch in the other hand. "Oh, Dick! Dave!"

But up the road there sounded no answer. Looking utterly worried, Reade came back into camp.

"I don't like the looks of this, fellows," he announced. "There's something wrong. Something has happened to one or both of the fellows. They left here before eight o'clock, and now it's twenty minutes of eleven. If everything had been all right, they'd have been back here by half-past nine o'clock at the latest."

"Suppose we haul down the tent, pack the outfit and move on down the road, looking for some trace of them," proposed Greg.

"No; that would delay the start too much," Tom replied, with a shake of his head. "Whoever goes out to hunt for Dick and Dave must move fast and not be tied to a horse and wagon. I'm going, for one. Who will go with me?"

"I will," promptly answered Dan, Harry and Greg, all

H. Irving Hancock

in one breath.

"We'll have to leave one fellow to watch the camp," Reade answered, with a shake of his head. "Hazy, I'm afraid the lot will have to fall to you."

"I'd rather go with you," Hazelton declared.

"Of course you would," Tom assented. "But at least one good man must stay here and look after our outfit. So you stay, Harry, and Dan and Greg will go with me."

"Going to take the lantern?" asked Greg, jumping up.

"Yes," Tom nodded, "but we won't light it unless we need it. Just for finding our footing at some dark part of the road the electric flash light will do."

Full of anxiety the trio set out on their search.

But in the meantime, what of Dick and Dave?

Theirs had been a busy evening. After the first rough pummeling, which left them breathless and sore, the tramp who had directed the rough work turned to his friends of the road.

"These young gents have furnished us with some exercise," he grinned wickedly. "Now, suppose we make 'em supply us with a little amusement?"

"It's risky, close to the road," returned one of the tramps who had been back in the shadows. "We don't know when someone will come along and butt in on our sport."

"Two of our crowd can go out as scouts," replied the ringleader.

"They'd better," nodded the adviser, "and even then we'd better take the cart, the old man and these young gents further back into the woods."

Neither Dick nor Dave had said anything so far, for they were too sore, and too much exhausted.

At the leader's command two men went down to the road, to watch in both directions.

"Give the whistle - you know the one - if anyone comes along that's likely to spoil the fun," was the ringleader's order.

Reuben Hinman had been deprived of the last dollar in money that he had with him. Quaking and subdued, the old man obeyed the order to mount his cart and drive the rig farther into the woods.

"Take the young gents along, and see that they behave themselves," directed the ringleader.

Dick and Dave did not yet feel in condition to offer any resistance or defiance. Even with the two "scouts" out on the road there were still six of the tramps left to take care of them.

The odds looked too heavy for another fight it when the last one had been so unsuccessful.

As Dick and Dave got to their feet and started along, followed and watched by the tramps, Dick tottered closer to his companion, managing to whisper:

"We've got to gain time, Dave. Pretend to be weak - crippled - badly hurt."

That was all. Prescott fell away again without his whisper having been detected by their captors.

Before quitting the spot near the road the ringleader had scattered the campfire so effectually that the embers would soon die out.

A full eighth of a mile back from the road the order was given to Hinman to rein in his horse.

"We're far enough from the road, now, so that we ain't likely to be spotted," said the boss tramp. "Now, let's see what these young gents can do to amuse us. Maybe they know how to sing and dance."

But Dick had sunk wearily to the ground, forcing his breath to come in rapid gasps.

"Get up there, younker," ordered the boss tramp.

"You've hurt me," moaned Dick, speaking the truth, though trying to convey a stronger impression than the facts would warrant.

"And we may hurt you more if you don't get cheerful and help make the evening pass pleasantly," sneered the boss tramp harshly.

"Wait till I - get so - I can get my breath - easier," begged Dick pantingly.

The boss turned to Darrin.

"Young fellow, wot can you do in the entertaining line?" demanded the fellow leeringly.

"Nothing," Dave retorted sulkily. "After you've kicked a fellow so that he's so sore he can scarcely move, do you expect him to do a vaudeville turn right away?"

"Get 'em on their feet," ordered the boss tramp. "We'll show 'em a few things!"

But Dick protested dolefully, sinking back to the ground as soon as the tramp who had hold of him showed a little compassion by letting go of his arm.

"Give me time, I tell you," Dick insisted in a weak voice. "Don't try to kill us, on top of such a thrashing as you gave us."

"Let go of me," urged Darry still speaking sulkily. "If you want anything better than a sob song you'll have to give me time to get my breath back."

As though satisfied that they could get no sport out of the high school boys for the present, the tramps allowed them to lie on the ground, breathing fitfully and groaning.

Dick was watching his chance to get up and bolt, depending upon his speed as a football player to take him out of this dangerous company. Darrin was equally watchful - but so were the tramps. Plainly the latter did not intend to let their prey get away from them easily.

As for Reuben Hinman, obeying a command, the peddler had alighted from his wagon and now sat with

H. Irving Hancock

his back against a tree. He had no thought of trying to get away, well knowing that his aged legs would not carry him far in a dash for freedom. The peddler's wearied horse stood and dozed between the shafts.

"It's about time for you younkers to be doing something," urged the boss tramp, after some minutes had slipped away.

"If you'll find the strength for me to stand up," urged Dick, "maybe I can dance, or do something."

"Did we muss you up as much as that?" demanded the boss tramp. "It serves you right, then. You shouldn't have meddled in our pastimes. Maybe it was all right for you fellers to get your horse and wagon back this morning, but you shouldn't have meddled to-night."

"I guess maybe that's right," nodded Darrin sulkily, "but you went in too strong in getting even. You had no call to cripple us for life."

"Oh, I guess it ain't as bad as that," muttered the boss tramp, though there was uneasiness in his voice.

So the tramps sat and smoked about a fire that one of their number had lighted. Another fifteen minutes went by.

"Come, it's time for you fellers to get busy, and give us something - songs, dances, comic recitations, or something like that. That's what we brought you here for," declared the boss, rising and prodding Darrin with one foot.

But Dave gave forth no sign. His eyes were half open,

yet he appeared to see nothing.

"Here, what have you been doing to my friend?" demanded Dick, crawling as if feebly over to where Darry lay. "Great Scott! You haven't injured him, have you?"

Dick acted his part as well as Dave did, but the boss tramp was not inclined to be nervous.

"No," he retorted shortly. "We haven't done much to either of you young fellers not a quarter as much as we're going to do if you don't both of you quit your nonsense soon. Help 'em up, now."

Dick allowed himself to be lifted to his feet and supported in a standing position by one of the most powerful-looking of the tramps. Darrin, however, continued to act as if he were almost lifeless.

"Give him the water cure," ordered the boss tramp, in an undertone to one of his confederates.

Going to the peddler's wagon the one so directed took down a pail. He went off in the darkness, but soon came back with a pail of water. Slipping up slyly, he dashed the water full in Darry's face.

With a gasping cry of rage Dave Darrin started to spring to his feet. Then, remembering his part, he sank back again to the ground.

"Raise him," directed the boss tramp. "He'll find his legs and stand on 'em. We are not going to let this show wait any longer!"

H. Irving Hancock

So Dave was roughly jerked to his feet. He swayed with pretended dizziness, next tottered to a tree, throwing his arms around it.

"You start something!" ordered the boss tramp of Prescott.

Feeling that now the chance might come for both of them to make a break for liberty, Dick answered, with a sheepish grin:

"If I can get wind enough I'll see if I can do an Indian war song and dance."

"Go ahead with it," ordered the boss. "It sounds good."

Once, three or four years ago, Dick had heard and seen such a war song and dance done at an Indian show in the summer time.

"I'll see if I can remember it," he replied.

Crooning in guttural tones, he started a swaying motion of his body. Gradually the unmelodious noise rose in volume. Brandishing his hands as though they contained weapons, he circled about the tree, gradually drawing nearer to Darrin.

"That song is mighty poor stuff," growled one of the tramps.

"Ready, Dave! Make a swift break for it!" whispered Prescott.

CHAPTER X

REUBEN HINMAN PROVES HIS METTLE

Uttering a loud whoop, Dick pushed Dave lightly.

At the same instant both young football players gathered for the spring, then started to speed away.

But they had had no chance to be quick enough, for some of the tramps had moved closer.

Both fugitives were seized, and now the battle was on again - two boys against overwhelming odds.

Right at the outset, however, a new note sounded.

"Go into it!" roared Tom Reade's voice. "Give 'em an old-fashioned high school drubbing."

Three more figures hurled themselves into the fray. And now, indeed, the battle raged. On the part of the high school boys there was no longer any thought of retreat, though it was still a matter of six men against five lads.

In the excitement of their friends' arrival, Dick and Dave were able to wrench themselves free.

H. Irving Hancock

Though those on the defense were boys, they were boys of good size, whose muscles had been hardened by regular training, as well as by grilling work on the football field.

Reade, in his first onset, hit one of the tramps such a blow that the fellow went to earth, where, though conscious, he preferred to remain for a while. Then it was five against five. But Dan soon got in a belt-line blow that put another tramp out of the fight.

From the road the two scouts ran up. When they saw, however, how the fight was going, they slunk off.

It was soon all but over. The boss tramp, however, armed with a club, crept up behind Prescott, aiming a savage blow at his head.

The blow would have landed, but for a new interruption.

With a cry that was more of a scream of alarm, old Reuben Hinman threw himself forward into the fray. Both his lean arms were wrapped around the tramp's legs.

Down came the tramp, just as Dick wheeled, falling heavily across Reuben Hinman, knocking the breath from the peddler.

Tom and Dave seized the boss tramp, as he tried to get up, hurling him back to the earth and sitting upon him.

"Let me up! Lemme go!" yelled the tramp.

"Keep cool," advised Tom. "You're likely to stay with

us a while."

"Don't let him go," cried Prescott. "That wretch has all of Mr. Hinman's money in his pockets."

"He'll give it up, then," guessed Reade.

"Come back here, you men!" roared the boss tramp, finding that all his fellows had fled.

"Call 'em all you want," mocked Reade. "They won't come back. They're too wise for that."

Dick, having given the order for the holding of the one tramp who remained, now gave all his attention to Reuben Hinman.

"The poor old man must be rather badly hurt," Prescott declared. "I can't get him to talk. Did you fellows bring a lantern with you?"

The lantern was lit and brought forward.

"I don't know what the matter is with him," said Dick at last. "But that's all the more reason why we must get him where he can have attention. The village of Dunfield is four miles below here. We must get him there at once. And we'll march the hobo there, too, in the hope that the village has a lock-up."

"It hasn't," snarled the tramp.

"Oh, we wouldn't take your word on a vital point like that," jeered Darry.

"The first thing you'll do will be to give back this poor

old man's money," Dick went on, eyeing the tramp.

"I haven't got it," came the prompt denial. "I turned it over to Joe and Bill, and they've got away with it."

"You're not going to like us a bit, my man," smiled Prescott. "We are not the kind of fellows to take your word for anything. We're going to see whether or not you have the money. We're going through your clothing for it. Poor old Mr. Hinman will need it for the care that I am afraid he is going to require. Search the fellow, Tom."

Greg now aided Dave in holding the vagabond. The tramp made such a commotion during the search that Dick and Greg added their help in holding him.

Out of a trousers' pocket Tom dragged the peddler's money sack. It was still tied.

"Let me have it," said Dick, and took it over by the campfire, where he untied the sack and peered into it.

"There's a roll of bills and at least ten, dollars in change in the sack," Dick announced, "so I think that none of the money has been taken."

"That's my money you've got," snarled the tramp.

"Tell that to the Senate!" Tom suggested.

Greg and Dan now aided Dick in lifting Mr. Hinman to the floor of his wagon, where they laid him on a pile of rags. Mr. Hinman was breathing, and his pulse could be distinctly felt.

"Dave, I guess you and I had better go along with the wagon," Dick suggested. "Now, see here, Tom, you and the other fellows go back to camp and act just as if we were all there. Start in the morning, as usual. You ought to be in Fenton by noon to-morrow. If Dave and I don't join you before that time, then you'll find us at Fenton."

"What are you going to do with the hobo?" Reade wanted to know.

"Roll him over on his face and tie his hands. Then we'll hitch him to the back of Mr. Hinman's wagon, and I'll walk with him and see that he goes along without making trouble, while Dave drives."

At this moment Reade alone was occupied in sitting on the captive, Dave having risen when it was suggested that he go with Dick to Dunfield.

"Here - quick!" yelled Reade, as the boss tramp gave a sudden heave.

But like a flash the hobo sprang up and darted off through the darkness. Tom, Dave and Dan started in swift pursuit, but the tramp soon doubled on his pursuers in the darkness and got away.

"Let him go," counseled Dick. "We've enough else to occupy our attention."

So Greg ran out to pass the word to the pursuers to discontinue the chase. Tom, when he returned, was very angry.

"You'd no business to leave the fellow like that,

Darry," he growled, "and I was a big fool not to be better on my guard. That fellow will make trouble for us yet - see if he doesn't."

"There was no use in chasing him any further, if he eluded you in the darkness," Dick remarked. "Dave, you get up on the wagon beside Mr. Hinman. I'll drive his horse."

Only as far as the road did Tom Reade, Dan and Greg accompany them, going ahead with the lantern to show the way.

"Now, you know the plan, Tom," Dick called quietly. "Fenton - at noon to-morrow."

"Good luck to you two!" called Reade. "And keep your eyes open for trouble."

"It will be someone else's trouble, if we meet any," laughed Darrin gayly.

"I wonder how it was that Tom and the other fellows didn't run into one of the scouts that the tramps had out," said Dick, after they had driven a short distance.

"Tom told me that they did catch a glimpse of a scout prowling by the road side, so they went around him," Darrin replied. "They slipped past the fellow without his seeing them."

As Dick held the reins he also eyed the dark road closely as they went along. He was not blind to the fact that the tramps might reassemble and rush the wagon, for these vagabonds would want both the peddler's money and what they would consider suitable revenge on the high school boys, for their part in the night's doings.

However, the village of Dunfield was reached without further adventure. Dave woke up the head of a family living in one of the cottages, and from him learned where to find the local physician. Then Dick drove to the medical man's house.

Dr. Haynes came downstairs at the first ring of the door bell, helping the boys to bring the still unconscious peddler inside.

There, under a strong light, with the peddler stretched on an operating table, the physician looked Reuben Hinman over.

"I can't find evidence of any bones being broken," said the physician. "It's my opinion that shock and exhaustion have done their work. Reuben is a very hard-working old man."

"Then you know him?" Dick asked.

"Everyone in this part of the country knows Reuben," replied the doctor. "He's one of our characters."

"He must have a hard life of it, and make rather a poor living," Prescott suggested.

"I guess he would make a good enough living, if -" began the physician, then checked himself.

"Are you going to bring the man to consciousness, doctor?" asked Dave.

"Yes; after I get a few things ready. I don't believe we'll have much trouble with him, though we'll have to get Reuben home and make him rest for a few days."

"Where does he live?" Dick inquired.

"In Fenton. Reuben has a queer little old home of his own there."

"Has he a wife?" Dick asked.

"She died fifteen years ago."

"Are there any children to look after Mr. Hinman?" Darry asked.

"He has children, but - well, they don't live with him," replied Dr. Haynes, as though not caring to discuss the subject.

Then the physician went to work over the peddler, who presently opened his eyes.

"Drink some of this," ordered the physician. "Now, you begin to feel better, don't you, Reuben?"

"Yes; and I've got to get up right away and see what I can do about getting back my money," cried the peddler.

"Don't try to get up just yet," ordered Dr. Haynes.

"If your money is worrying you, Mr. Hinman, I have it," Dick broke in, showing the sack.

A cry of joy escaped the peddler. He sank back, murmuring:

"You're good boys! I knew you were good boys!"

"You take the money, Doctor, if you please, and turn it over to Mr. Hinman when he's able to count it," urged Prescott, handing the sack to their host.

"Now, Mr. Hinman will want to sleep a little while, so we'll go outside and chat, if you've nothing pressing to do," suggested the physician.

Dick and Dave thought they might learn more about the odd peddler, but Reuben Hinman's affairs was one subject that the physician did not seem inclined to talk about.

"Now, if you young men want to take Reuben over to Fenton," said Dr. Haynes, at last, "I'll telephone Dr. Warren from here, and he'll be expecting you. It'll take you about two hours to get over to Fenton at the gait that old Reuben's horse travels."

This time a mattress was placed on top of the pile of rags, and the peddler was made as comfortable as possible for the trip.

"Remember, Reuben, you've got to stay in the house and take care of yourself for three or four days," was Dr. Haynes' parting injunction.

"I can't spare the time from my business," groaned the old man.

"You'll have to, this time, Reuben, as the means of

being ready to do more business. So be good about it. You have two fine lads taking care of you to-night."

"I know that, Doctor."

It was five o'clock in the morning when Dick and Dave drove into the main street of Fenton. Yet they found an automobile in the road, and Dr. Warren, a very young man, hailed them.

"Drive right along, boys. I'll show you the way to the house," called the Fenton physician.

It was a very small and very plain little house of five rooms into which Reuben was carried, but it was a very neatly kept little house.

Reuben Hinman was put to bed and made as comfortable as possible.

"Are there any relatives to take care of this man?" Dick asked.

"There are relatives," replied Dr. Warren, with an odd smile, "but I guess we won't ask any of them to care for Reuben. There are a couple of good women among the neighbors, and I'll call them to come over here soon."

It was after six in the morning when Dr. Warren left the peddler, with two motherly looking women to take care of him.

Dr. Warren, after some conversation with the boys, returned to his home.

"As this is where we're going to meet Tom and the other fellows," said Dick, "I propose that we see if we can find a restaurant and have something to eat. Then we'll try to hire a couple of beds and leave a call for noon. I'm both hungry and fagged out."

They found the restaurant without difficulty, and also succeeded in hiring two cots in an upstairs room over the restaurant.

"Reuben Hinman is becoming a good deal of a puzzle to me," murmured Dave Darrin, as the chums ate their breakfast.

"He's almost a man of mystery," agreed Dick, "though not quite, except to us. I imagine that these Fenton people know all about our peddler friend."

"Both doctors seemed to know a lot about the old man," remarked Dave thoughtfully. "Yet it was strange; neither of them would really tell us anything definite about Mr. Hinman."

"If doctors told all they know about people." smiled Dick, "I believe that life would become exciting for a while, but before long there would be fewer doctors in the world than there are now."

At just twelve o'clock Dick and Dave were called. They sprang up, somewhat drowsy, yet on the whole greatly refreshed. After washing they dressed and went forth in search of their camp outfit and friends.

H. Irving Hancock

CHAPTER XI

TOM IDEALIZES WORKING CLOTHES

After the reunion at Fenton the high school boys enjoyed many days of "hiking" and of all-around good times, yet nothing happened in that interval that requires especial chronicling.

Nor in that time did Dick & Co. hear any more of Reuben Hinman, as they were now some distance from Fenton.

"We'll make Ashbury to-night," Dick announced one morning. "We'll go about two miles past the town, halt there for two or three days' rest, and then - back to good old Gridley for ours."

"Gridley's all right. Fine old town," Tom declared. "But as for me, I wish we didn't have to go back there for another two months, instead of feeling that we have to be there in a fortnight from now."

"This has been a great hike," Dick agreed, "and a fortnight of life of a kind that has had nothing but joy in it. Yet we've the years ahead to think of, haven't we?"

"What has that got to do with going back to Gridley?"

demanded Danny Grin.

"Well, what are we going to the high school for?" questioned Dick Prescott.

"I'm going because the folks send me," Dan declared. "Can't help myself."

"Don't you want to get anywhere in life?"

"I suppose I do," Dalzell assented half dubiously.

"Danny boy, I'm ashamed of you," Dick exclaimed, though his eyes were smiling. "Are you content, Dan, to grow up and use your fine muscles in performing the duties of a day laborer?"

"Not exactly," Dan answered.

"You'd rather be president of a big railroad company?"

"Yes, if I had to choose between the two jobs."

"Then perhaps you can get a glimmering of why you're in high school," Dick went on. "When you compare the railway president and the laborer, the difference between them lies a good deal in the difference in their natural abilities. Yet a lot depends, too, upon the difference in their training. You don't find many college graduates wielding the pick and shovel for a living, nor many high school graduates doing so, either. By the way, Dan, what are you going to do in life?"

Dalzell shook his head.

H. Irving Hancock

"Then within the next year you had better go after the problem and make your decision hard and fast. Fasten your gaze on something in life that you want, and then don't stop traveling until you get it, and it's all yours! A boy of seventeen, without an idea of what he intends to do in life has already turned down the lane that leads to the junk heap. Get out of that road, Danny!"

"What are you going to do in life yourself?" challenged Danny Grin.

"I'm going to West Point if there's any possible chance of my winning the nomination from our home district. There's a vacancy to be competed for next spring."

"Some smarter boy may win it away from you," Danny Grin retorted.

"He'll have to hustle, then," Dick rejoined, his eyes flashing.

"But suppose you do lose the nomination and can't go to West Point - what will you do then?"

"I have plans, in case I can't get to West Point," Prescott answered quietly. "However, as yet I won't admit the defeat of my West Point ambition."

"I'd try for West Point myself, if it weren't for Dick being in the way," Greg declared. "But I never could get past Dick in an exam."

"If you want it, come on and try," begged Dick. "Our Congressman gives the nomination to the boy in the district who can stand up best under an exam. Go in and try for it, Greg! Work like a horse when high school opens. You might get it."

"And take it away from you?" blurted Holmes.

"If you can get it from me, you ought to do it, Holmesy. The best men are needed in every walk of life. I'll promise, in advance, not to be 'sore' if you can win it away from me."

"Yes! I'd try all winter," scoffed Greg, "and then in the end some sad-eyed fellow from a back-country village would bob up and win it away from us both."

"Let the sad-eyed fellow have it, if he is the better man," Dick agreed heartily. "But fear of defeat isn't going to hold me back. Don't let it stop you, either, Greg!"

"It's going to be Annapolis for mine - the United States Naval Academy and a commission in the United States Navy!" Darry declared, his eyes snapping.

"I'd rather like that, too," Danny Grin declared.

"Then go after it," urged Dick Prescott. "Get some real plan in your mind of what you're going to do in life, and then follow that plan, night and day, until you either win or drop from exhaustion."

"Wouldn't I be a funny-looking lamb in a midshipman's uniform?" queried Dalzell blinking fast.

"No funnier looking than any of the rest of us," Dick retorted. "Now, Tom isn't talking much, but we all know what he's going to do, for he has already been working at it. He has been studying surveying, for he

H. Irving Hancock

means to make a great civil engineer of himself one of these days."

"And I'm going into the game with him," declared Hazelton.

"That's because you've always had Tom about to tell you what to do, and to keep you from butting your head into things in the dark," jeered Danny Grin. "Hazy, you're going to become an engineer just because you shiver at the thought of trying to do anything in life without having old Tommy Long-legs to advise you when to wash your face or come in out of the rain."

"Harry is a pretty bright surveyor already," Tom declared. "He has been keeping mum about it, but Harry can go out into the country with a transit and run up the field notes for a map about as handily as the next kid in his teens."

"I should think you'd like the Army or the Navy, Tom," mused Dalzell aloud.

"Nothing doing," Reade retorted. "I want to be one of the big and active men of the world, who do big things. I want to map out the wilderness. I want to dam the raging flood and drive the new railroad across the desert. I want to construct. I want to work day and night when the big deeds are to be done. That's why I wouldn't care for the Army or Navy; it's too idle a life."

"An idle life!" exclaimed Dick and Dave in the same breath.

"Yes," Tom went on dryly. "Did you ever see an Army or a Navy officer?"

"I've seen several of them," Dick replied, "and have talked with some of them."

"Same here," added Darrin.

"Did you see the officers in uniform?" Reade pressed.

"Yes, of course -" said Prescott.

"Their uniforms were nice and neat, weren't they?" Tom asked.

"Of course," Prescott answered.

"Then that was because your Army or Navy officers hadn't been doing any hard work that would ruffle the neatness of their uniforms," finished Tom triumphantly, "and there you are! I can dress up on Sundays or holidays, but on the work days, when I'm a civil engineer, I want to wear clothes that show that I'm not afraid to tackle the rough and hard things of life."

"Then you might join Dan in being a day laborer," teased Dick laughingly.

"Oh, no! I want to use my brain along with my muscles, and that's why I'm going to be a civil engineer."

"Army a Navy officers may have had an easy time of it once," Dave went on warmly, but times have changed. Our fighting men, to-day, are obliged to hustle all the time to keep up with the march and progress of

H. Irving Hancock

science. I asked an Army officer, once, what he did in his spare time. He looked at me rather queerly, then replied, 'I sleep.'"

"He was lazy as well as offensively neat, then," laughed Tom. "As for me, I enjoy my old clothes, and that is one of the reasons why I'm having so much fun out of this trip. I don't have to dress up!"

"You'd feel first rate if you could be dressed up for a few hours, go into a hotel dining room, have a good meal and then slip into a ballroom for a dance," laughed Prescott.

"Bosh!" flared Tom. "I'm no dandy, and all I want is to be a man."

"How do you stand, Harry?" grinned Dave Darrin. "Do you agree with Tom that dirt is the best stuff with which to decorate one's clothing?"

"I never said that," broke in Tom hotly. "I'm as ready for a bath and clean clothing as any of you. I like to wear old clothes - not soiled ones!"

"If anyone happens to overhear us talking," laughed Hazy, "he'll think that we're all planning to take up prize fighting as our work in life."

"I don't like to hear the officers of the Army and Navy scoffed at as a lot of idling, time-wasting dandies," Darry asserted.

"And I don't like to be accused of liking dirt on my clothes, just because I am going to be a civil engineer," Tom explained in a milder voice.

An ideal bit of green forest, at the edge of a limpid lake, appealed to Dick & Co. as the noon stopping place.

"I've a good mind to fish," remarked Danny Grin.

"Go ahead, if you want to," Dick assented, "but we've got a lot of fresh meat that we simply must cook this noon, for it may not keep until night."

"It would take you an hour or more, even though the fish bit readily, to catch enough fish to feed this little multitude," Tom remarked.

"I don't want to wait that long for my meal to-day."

"I don't believe I want to wait, either," Dalzell agreed, and gave up the idea of fishing.

Luncheon went on in record time that morning. It was not later than half-past eleven o'clock when they sat down to the meal, and but a few minutes past noon when the dishes were stacked up, ready to be washed.

"Whizz-zz!" whistled Dave, as the sounds made by a swiftly driven automobile reached their ears. "Someone is hurrying to get his noon meal. Just hear that old spurt wagon throb!"

The boys sat some hundred feet in from the highway. The automobile did not interest them much until -

Bang!

Then the car stopped with a scraping sound.

"Gracious!" exclaimed Danny Grin, jumping up at the sound of the explosion. Then he sat down once more, looking sheepish.

"Give up the Annapolis bee, Danny boy," laughed Tom. "That was nothing but a tire blowing out. If you got into the Navy, and a fourteen-inch gun went off when you weren't expecting it, you'd be half way to the planet Neptune before your comrades could call you back."

"How easily we make light of other people's troubles," mused Prescott.

"What makes you say that?" asked Darrin.

"Why, for instance, that party down in the road has been stopped by a blown-out tire. Probably they were in a hurry to get somewhere, too. Now, they're delayed perhaps a half an hour, but it doesn't give us a flicker of concern."

"It interests me, anyway," Reade announced, rising. "Anything in the mechanical line does. It may even be that the man driving that car doesn't know just how to put on a new tire. I'm going to saunter down and see."

Five members of Dick & Co. didn't take the trouble even to glance keenly at the halted car.

Tom took a dozen steps, then suddenly shouted back:

"Fellows, your indifference will vanish, now. Look who's here!"

CHAPTER XII

TROUBLE WITH THE RAH-RAH-RAHS

A broad-shouldered man, his back to Dick & Co., was assisting a middle-aged woman to alight from the car.

As Tom's voice reached their ears five girls exclaimed in delight, then began to wave their hands in most friendly fashion.

Dick & Co. were on the run by this time, for the broad-shouldered man was Dr. Bentley, the woman Mrs. Bentley, and the five girls Laura Bentley, Belle Meade, Susie Sharp, Clara Marshall and Anita Murray.

"Hm! Young men, I'm beginning to feel annoyed," remarked Dr. Bentley with pretended severity, though he shook hands pleasantly enough with the boys. "Whenever Mrs. Bentley and I take some of Laura's friends for a spin anywhere you appear to have our route and you bob up on the map."

"Then we'll withdraw, sir, at once," Dick suggested.

"No, you won't," retorted the doctor. "Young Reade is engaged, on the spot, to help me fit on a new tire. Perhaps Hazelton will help. The rest of you may disappear, and take the ladies with you, if you will.

Yet, really, it looks as though you learn our route and follow it."

"That isn't fair, doctor," Dave rejoined. "We're on foot, and have been away from Gridley for something over a fortnight. It is you who must have been following us, with that seven-passenger automobile of yours. And may I remind you, sir, that you wouldn't have bursted the tire if you hadn't been driving at something under a hundred and eighty miles an hour in the effort to overtake us?"

"I'm beaten", laughed Dr. Bentley. "I take it all back. I agree that the appearances are all against me. But I didn't know that you young scions of Gridley were on the road. I was driving fast in order to bring the ladies to Ashbury in time for luncheon. And now, they won't get it."

"Small loss to them, and great gain to us," smiled Dick. "We have provisions enough in our wagon to offer all the luncheon that your party can possibly care to eat."

"No, no! We've encroached upon your hospitality too often in the past," replied Dr. Bentley, with a shake of his head. "We won't be delayed long. Just how long, Reade, do you think it is going to take us to fit on the new tire?"

"The car ought to be ready to run again in fifteen minutes," Tom answered truthfully.

"And we can make Ashbury in another fifteen minutes," Laura's father continued. "So we won't rob the pantry of Dick & Co. to-day."

Dick and three of his chums conducted Mrs. Bentley and the five high school girls in under the trees. Of course the girls wanted to see the outfit, though it was now packed on the wagon.

"Are you going far, this trip?" Dick inquired.

"Ashbury will be the end of our run," Mrs. Bentley answered.

"And of ours, too," Dick nodded. "We agreed to that this morning."

"But we are to stay at Ashbury two or three days," Laura added. "Dad has been making arrangements for us at the hotel there, and he calls it a fine summer place. We know some people who are stopping there now, so we are going to have a pleasant little time of it, I expect. When do you reach Ashbury, Dick?"

"To-night," Prescott answered.

"Mother," Laura went on, "aren't you going to invite the boys to luncheon at the hotel tomorrow?"

"I shall be delighted to do so, if they will accept," replied Mrs. Bentley smiling.

"We'd cause a sensation in the hotel, wouldn't we?" laughed Danny Grin, looking down ruefully at his dusty "hike clothes."

"You have other clothing with you, haven't you?" asked Susie Sharp.

"Nothing better than what we're wearing now,"

H. Irving Hancock

Greg replied.

"Come, just the same, anyway," urged Mrs. Bentley. "You boys are on a rough trip, and you're not expected to have large wardrobes with you. So I shall expect you all at the Ashbury Terraces by noon to-morrow."

"And there's to be a dance there to-morrow night," Belle continued, a trifle mischievously. "Of course, you will come to the dance."

"Yes - if you invite us!" Dick took up the challenge thus unexpectedly.

"Then you're surely invited," laughed Susie Sharp. "Aren't they, Mrs. Bentley?"

"Yes; if they promise to come," agreed the doctor's wife. "And, perhaps, they would rather dine than lunch with us, and then they can attend the dance after dinner."

"That would be much better, thank you," Dick replied gratefully.

But the other fellows eyed him askance, in wondering amazement. What on earth could Dick mean by accepting for himself and chums a dinner and dance invitation when they had nothing to wear save their road-worn and travel-stained hiking clothes?

"Dick is getting careless - making such an engagement for us for to-morrow evening," Tom confided to Hazelton, when the news was related to him.

"Well, you won't need to mind, anyway," laughed

Harry gleefully. "You, of all fellows, can't kick, Tom, after the way you've been glorifying life in one's working clothes."

Dr. Bentley was delighted to have such capable young men as Reade and Hazelton on hand to put on the new tire, for the man of medicine, though a clever surgeon in some lines, was but little of a machinist. He worked with finer tools than those that his repair box carried.

Twenty minutes later the new tire was on and had been pumped up.

"All ready!" sang out Tom.

"You might have dallied longer on that job," Dick answered reproachfully.

"Are you anxious to keep us hungry girls away from our luncheon that much longer?" cried Susie Sharp.

"Well, whose fault is it that you are not having your luncheon, here and now?" smiled Prescott. "You didn't like our cooking, though."

"Don't I?" chirped Miss Sharp. "If it weren't for making you vainer than you are, Dick Prescott, I'd tell you that the trout luncheon you gave us at the second lake still lingers in our memories."

Regretfully, the boys escorted the high school girls down to the road, assisting them and Mrs. Bentley into the car.

"To-morrow evening, then!" called Mrs. Bentley. "Be at the hotel by half-past five o'clock, won't you?"

"Without fail," Dick smiled back, "unless circumstances beyond our control prevent us."

Good-byes were eagerly called, Dr. Bentley warmly expressing his thanks to Reade and Hazelton for their assistance. Then, with a warning honk, the big car started away.

Then all hands turned upon Dick. "Prescott, why on earth did you let us in for a dinner and dance tomorrow night?" quivered Greg.

"Look at us - the only outside clothes we have with us!" exploded Danny Grin.

"We're frights!" chimed in Dave.

"We'll disgrace the girls," blurted Tom, "unless in the meantime we can find some real tramps with whom to trade clothes."

"We'll feel ashamed enough to drop, when we get among civilized folks," moaned Harry.

"This is a fine chance to prove or disprove Tom's theory that a fellow ought to feel most at home in his old working clothes," chuckled Dick.

"Was that why you did it - accepted that dinner and dance invitation?" gasped Dave.

"Partly," laughed Prescott.

"I won't go!" flared Reade, his face showing red under its heavy coat of tan.

"Oh, yes, you will," Dick insisted, "or else admit that you perjured yourself when you idealized your working duds this morning."

"And are you really going to-morrow night?" Greg insisted.

"I certainly am," young Prescott affirmed.

That was too much of a poser for the other members of Dick & Co. Nothing more was said on the subject, though the five boys did considerable thinking.

Toward five o'clock they came in sight of Ashbury. A few minutes later they had reached a point where the highway turned into one of the streets of the town.

Here a uniformed bell-boy from the Ashbury Terraces Hotel approached them.

"Is Mr. Prescott in this party?" he inquired.

"That's my name," Dick answered.

"Then I am requested by Dr. Bentley to guide you to a camping place inside the Terraces' grounds," replied the bell-boy. "Dr. Bentley has arranged it with the manager."

This was a surprise, indeed, but Dick & Co. followed their guide, who turned in through a gate at some distance from the handsome summer hotel. Their guide led them to a grove on a broad terrace, from which the high school lads had an excellent view of one of the porches of the hotel.

"Look at the smartly dressed people over there!" groaned Greg, as soon as the bell-boy had left them. "Look at those girls, in their gowns of white lace! Look at the fellows over there, in flannels and white duck! Look at -"

"Shut up!" commanded Tom hoarsely. "Don't rub it in."

"Dick," suggested Darry, with some bitterness, "we'll feel like princes in our flannel shirts and khaki leggings, won't we?"

"I've an idea," offered Danny Grin. "By way of dressing up we can leave off our khaki leggings and give our trousers an extra brushing all around. We'll look quite respectable, after all!"

"Gentlemen," remarked Tom Reade solemnly, "I have the honor to make a motion to the effect that Messrs. Darrin, Holmes and Dalzell be appointed a committee of three to take Dick Prescott away and drown him in the nearest sizable body of water!"

"Carried!" proclaimed Hazelton.

Instead, however, all hands fell to work putting up the tent and preparing for supper.

"Rah, rah, rah!" rose joyously on the air. Then, out of the woods behind the camp appeared eight young men in multi-colored raiment. Gorgeous bands surrounded their straw hats; their blazer coats resembled so many rainbows. Yet, apart from their coats of many colors, these young men were smartly dressed, and it was plain that they carried with them considerable of an estimate of their own importance. Their average age appeared to be about twenty-one years.

"Rah, rah, rah!" rang the chorus again. Then one of the eight, moving in advance of The others, called back:

"Fellows, what have we here?"

"Gipsies!" called another.

"Plain hoboes!" from a third.

"It's a gang of juvenile desperadoes escaped from some reformatory," declared a fourth.

"Rah, rah, rah!"

With noisy yells the eight young men descended upon the camp.

"Don't you think you'd better steer off?" called Dave, putting himself as much as he could in their way.

"Why, it talks!" cried one of the rah-rah-rah fellows, in mock astonishment.

"Just like a human being!" added a third.

"Wonder what these animals are doing here?" propounded another.

So they invaded the camp, poking their heads in at the tent entrance, examining the wagon with a good deal of curiosity, and poking into the boxes containing the food that Dick and Greg had just laid out with a view to starting preparations for supper.

H. Irving Hancock

"Now, gentlemen," called Dick, "if you think your curiosity has been sufficiently gratified, do you mind clearing out and letting us alone?"

A variety of mocking replies greeted that proposition.

"We don't like to be disagreeable, you understand," Dave hinted, "but, really, we begin to feel that we have had a great sufficiency of your company, gentlemen."

"What are you going to do about it?" demanded one of the eight intruders rather aggressively.

Dave Darrin doubled his fists, ready to fight, now, at any further provocation. Even good-natured Tom looked about for some sort of club. But Dick answered, coolly:

"What are we going to do? First of all, we are merely going to suggest for your consideration the idea that gentlemen don't remain where they're not wanted."

"Freshie!" yelled one of the eight contemptuously.

"Toss him in a blanket," advised another.

"We don't mind your presence as much as your bad manners," Dick remarked coldly. "Will you kindly take your leave?"

"No!" shouted three or four of their tormentors derisively.

Dave, his fists still clenched, bounded forward. One chap, in an especially brilliant blazer, reached out to box Darry on the ear.

That blow never landed, but the tormentor did - -on the earth.

"Eight rainbow hoboes,
Looking for life's leaven,
One bumped his eyelash,
And then there were but seven!"

improvised Danny Grin joyously.

"Clean out this camp!" yelled one of the others.

"Come on and do it, then!" yelled Tom Reade, losing all patience at last.

Dick & Co. suddenly presented a solid fighting rank that had accomplished great things on the gridiron. In this formation they advanced toward their tormentors.

There might have been an ugly clash, but one of the eight shouted:

"Come on, fellows! Don't tease the babies. They haven't had their warm milk yet."

Away darted the rainbow eight, Darrin's victim being on his feet by this time and foremost in the retreat.

"Rah, rah, rah!" came back on the air as the high school boys broke a formation for which they had no further need at present.

"Those fellows are plainly guests at the hotel, and we're going to have trouble with them yet," Prescott predicted wisely.

H. Irving Hancock

CHAPTER XIII

A SNUB AND THE QUICK RETORT

At half-past five o'clock the next day, Dick & Co. strolled up to the porch of the Ashbury Terraces Hotel.

From one of the parlors a cry of recognition in a girlish voice floated out. Then appeared the Gridley High School girls, with Susie Sharp in the lead.

"I thought you told us you didn't have any other than your hike clothing with you!" Susie cried accusingly to Tom Reade.

"We didn't. We told you the truth," Reade rejoined.

"Then these -"

"These new clothes were bought with money from the treasury," Reade informed her.

"Does our appearance suit you, ladies?" Greg asked smiling.

"You look like so many tailor's models," replied Belle Meade, adding, sweetly: "If that is any praise."

Certainly Dick & Co., clad in well-fitting white duck

suits, presented a creditable appearance.

"We've been preparing our friends at the Terraces for a different looking lot of young men," laughed Susie. "We have told them that a number of high school boy friends of ours were coming over to dinner and the hop attired in the same clothes they have been wearing in camp and on the road. Now we must apologize to them for presenting fashion plates."

The explanation, as Dick presently furnished it to Laura Bentley, was a simple one. Dick had been handling the funds of the six boys on this expedition, which had held out much longer than any of his chums had known. At the time of accepting the invitation young Prescott had felt sure that an Ashbury clothier would be able to furnish proper clothes for his party, and his guess had proved a correct one. Moreover, the treasury of Dick & Co. had been easily able to endure the drain, for these white clothes had not been costly.

Mrs. Bentley presently joined the little Gridley group of young people on the veranda. That good lady noted, with secret pleasure, the well-groomed appearance of her young guests.

"Rah, rah, rah!" came boisterously up the veranda, as the camp visitors of the evening before suddenly appeared. "Rah, rah, rah!"

Then, halting in a compact group midway on the veranda, they shouted in chorus:

"S-A-U-N-D-E-R-S! Saunders! Saunders! Siss-boom-a-a-ah! Rah, rah, rah!"

"College boys!" exclaimed Susie Sharp in an impatient undertone. "College boys, and the worst of their kind. They're noisy nuisances!"

"So far as any other guest has been able to discover they haven't any manners," Belle added.

Then, espying the girls and their guests the rah-rah-rah boys came briskly up the veranda.

"Good evening, Miss Meade!" called one of them, lifting his hat. "Glorious evening, isn't it? How many dances may I have the honor of claiming at the hop to-night?"

Belle Meade blushed slightly and drew back a step, resenting the young man's familiarity.

In front of the presumptuous youth stepped Dave Darrin, with eyes flashing.

"Kindly keep your distance, young man!" Dave advised, in a tone of dangerous quiet.

"Who asked you to speak?" inquired the rah-rah youth mockingly.

"I am a friend of the young lady, and she finds your presence an intrusion," replied Darry, controlling himself by a mighty effort.

"All guests of the hotel are supposed to be acquainted," urged the rah-rah youth, reddening a trifle.

"These young ladies do not wish to recognize you and your friends as acquaintances," replied Dave. "Kindly efface yourselves!"

"Don't make your lack of breeding too conspicuous," Dick advised, in a quiet undertone, to another of the intruders who had pushed forward to join in the conversation.

A sudden sense of discomfort seemed to sweep over the eight presuming young men. They turned and moved away, though muttering among themselves.

"That is the kind of young men I thought they were," Laura observed. "I am glad that you boys sent them off about their own affairs."

Dr. Bentley joined the young people last of all.

"I have just returned from a long walk," he explained. "I have to make the most of these brief summer vacations of mine."

When dinner was announced, Dr. and Mrs. Bentley and the young people took seats at a long table reserved for their party.

It was a pleasant meal in the midst of an animated scene.

Over at another table the rah-rah boys made a good deal of noise until the head waiter went to them, uttering a few words in low tones. After that the rah-rah youngsters quieted down considerably.

A delightful half-hour stroll on the verandas followed the dinner. Then, like most of the guests, the Gridley young people drifted into the hotel ballroom where the musicians were playing a march.

Dick secured Mrs. Bentley for the first dance, as the doctor preferred to remain on the veranda. Then, after the first dance, a general change of partners was made.

But the Gridley boys were too well bred to claim all the dances with their girl friends. Laura and her friends had other acquaintances at the hotel. Dick & Co. stood back to give these other young men a fair opportunity of securing some dances with the girls.

It was eleven o'clock when the hop had finished. For a few moments Dick & Co. chatted with the Gridley High School girls on the porch. Then they prepared to take their leave.

"We've had a splendid time, for which we must thank you all," Dick declared. "We did not look for any such pleasant evening as this has been when we left home on our hike."

"We are indebted to you all for the most delightful time of our lives," Tom stated formally with a very low bow.

"We couldn't have had a nicer time under any circumstances. Thank you all," Dave Darrin said, on taking leave.

The other boys found words in which to fitly express their pleasure and gratitude.

Then, as Mrs. Bentley and the girls went in side the hotel, the Gridley High School boys wheeled to march back to camp.

"I wonder what the head waiter said to the rah-rah boys?" asked Reade curiously.

"I don't know, but I can guess the meaning of what he said," laughed Darry. "Did you ever see such an ill-bred lot of fellows before!"

"They're not college boys," Dick declared quietly. "I don't know where they came from, but certainly none of them have ever been through as much as a year in any real college."

"They're about as frisky as some college boys," retorted Danny Grin.

"College boys may be full of mischief, at times," Dick returned, "but at least they know how to behave well when they should do so. College men never think it funny to be rude with women, for instance. College men are usually the sons of well-bred parents, and they also acquire additional finish at college. Moreover, the English language is one of the subjects taught in colleges. These cheeky rah-rah boys were very slip-shod in their speech. I don't know who these fellows are, but they're not real college men."

"Say, it must be nice," remarked Hazelton, "to be able to travel about the country, stopping at such nice hotels. Laura and her friends manage to have pretty good times."

"Their families are all better off than ours, in a worldly sense," Dick replied. "When you stop to think of it, there are far more girls than boys in our good old high school who come from comfortable homes. Perhaps two dozen of our high school fellows come from

H. Irving Hancock

homes of considerable wealth. The rest of us don't. More than half of the Gridley High School girls come from families where servants are kept. I wonder if it is that way, generally, in the United States?"

Prescott had unwittingly stumbled upon a fact often noted. The homes of plain American wage earners send more boys than girls to high school. The well-to-do families send more of their boys to private schools, while their girls are more likely to attend high school.

However, as the boys neared their camp, all other thoughts were driven from their minds.

Tom Reade, who was leading, stopped abruptly, holding up one hand.

"Now, what do you think of anyone who would do a trick like that?" he demanded with a sharp in-drawing of his breath.

"The sneaks!" breathed Darry fiercely.

"Who could have done it?" gasped Greg.

For the tent was down - flat. The wagon lay on its side, nor was the horse anywhere in sight.

"Did those rascally tramps follow us and watch their chance?" demanded Dave Darrin hotly.

"I don't believe the tramps did it," spoke Prescott, in a very quiet voice, though an angry flush rose to his face. "I believe that we must look in a different direction for the offenders."

"The rah-rah hoodlums?" gasped Greg Holmes.

"Yes," Dick nodded.

H. Irving Hancock

CHAPTER XIV

DICK & CO. MAKE AN APPLE "PIE"

"Then I wish we had 'em here!" sputtered Tom Reade vengefully. "I could eat two of them at this moment, and without salt!"

"They need salting badly!" growled Dave Darrin angrily.

The tent was not only down. Each guy rope had been cut in the middle, so that the cordage could not be used again.

"I never saw anything more sneaking!" cried Reade in rage and disgust.

"Unless it will be the way that we shall sneak up behind the rah-rah crowd and square matters!" remarked Darry meaningly.

"First of all, we must be sure of their guilt," warned Dick. "It won't do to try to even up a score that's based only on suspicion. Wait until I get a lantern out of the wreck, and then we'll explore the ground to see if we can discover any real proof against the rascals."

"Let's get into our working clothes first," proposed

Reade. "We might want to wear these white clothes again before we get home."

So Tom and Dave held up a part of the canvas while Dick slipped in under the folds of the tent to find the box in which they had left their hike clothing.

"The box isn't here," Dick called. "Neither can I see any of the bedding."

"Get hold here, fellows, and lift up more of the canvas," Reade called.

"There isn't anything in the tent. All the stuff has been cleaned out." Prescott announced in a voice of disgust.

"It was the tramps, then," Dave declared. "The rah-rah boys wouldn't take the risk of stealing anything."

"Hold on! I've found a lantern," called Prescott. "I'll come out with that."

He appeared a moment later, lighting the lantern.

"Now, let's see what we can find," he urged. Not far away the high school boys came upon the prints of sharp-toed shoes.

"The tramps didn't wear shoes that would make these prints," declared Dick. "Neither do any of our crowd. Fellows, we owe our surprise to the rah-rah humorists."

"Then we'll pay 'em back in good measure," cried Darry in exasperation.

After some searching Dick & Co. came upon their clothes chest, at a distance of some hundred yards from camp. The chest had not been rifled, for it was locked and the key rested in Dick's pocket.

"Help me with it, Tom, and we'll carry it back," said Prescott in a low, hard tone. "We need our working clothes at once, for there is work to be done to-night!"

The needed change of costume was quickly made. Off came the white suits, which were carefully folded and put away. Then on went the khaki and flannel clothing.

"Dan, you stay with the tent," Dick ordered, with the air of a general. "Greg, you and Harry make it your main business to see if you can find the horse. The rest of us will concern ourselves with finding out whether the rah-rah fellows are still outside the hotel."

"Here's the horse - grazing," shouted Greg, two minutes later.

"Run back, Dave, and pilot Greg and Harry here, after they've staked the horse down," Prescott suggested. "We don't want to make too much noise, for our tormentors may yet be about somewhere."

"Hazy stumbled upon some of the blankets," Greg announced, when he and Harry joined Dave. "I don't believe any of our stuff has been carried off, Dick. It has just been scattered."

"Perhaps we'd better gather in all our camp stuff first, then," Dick decided. "We can't afford to lose any of our camp outfit."

Ten or fifteen minutes of searching, with the aid of the lantern, resulted in recovering all of their scattered possessions, even to the last of the cots, pillows and blankets.

"Now, let's make a sweep of the dark parts of the hotel grounds, and we may happen upon the rah-rahs, still chuckling over the fun they've had with us."

But the five boys had not gone far when they were stopped by a well-dressed young stranger of about twenty.

"Mr. Prescott?" asked the stranger.

"Yes," nodded Dick.

"I am one of the bell-boys at the hotel. When I went off duty I asked the manager's permission to change my uniform for citizen's clothing and watch those eight noisy fellows."

"The college boys?" asked Harry quickly.

"They're not college boys!" returned the young stranger. "They've been giving a fake Saunders yell, and that was what made me dislike them, for I've just finished the sophomore year at Saunders myself. I'm working at the Terraces as bell-boy to help pay next year's tuition at Saunders. The manager permitted me to watch those fellows, but somehow they got away from me. I got track of them again near to your camp. Just as I came along they were scooting away, but a glance showed me the mischief they had worked, so I followed them."

H. Irving Hancock

"Do you know where they are now?" Dick asked eagerly.

"I know where they were ten minutes ago," replied the bell-boy.

"Then please take us to them as quickly as you can," begged Darry vehemently. "I'm fairly aching to pass the time of night with them!"

"I'll do it," agreed the bell-boy. "Follow me, please."

"I wonder why they went to all that trouble to be so disagreeable to us," Prescott muttered, as the little party strode along.

"You had some dispute with that crowd, on the hotel porch to-night, didn't you?" asked the bell-boy.

"Yes; they tried to address some of our girl friends, whom they didn't know and we objected to their insolence."

"That was what made the rah-rah boys sore," went on the bell-boy. "I heard them talking about it before I left them. It seems, too, that the manager sent the head waiter to stop their nonsense in the dining room to-night. For some reason these sham college boys blame you fellows for that humiliation also. So they're chuckling over what they've done to your outfit to teach you to mind your own business, as they put it."

"I hope we catch up with 'em before they get back to the hotel," uttered Tom fervently. "But warn us, please, whenever we get so close that they're likely to hear our voices."

The bell-boy now led them through an orchard.

"There seem to be a lot of apples on the ground," remarked Prescott, halting.

"Green ones - they're no good," replied the bell-boy.

"Then they are good - just what we want!" ejaculated Prescott. "Hold on, fellows! Fill your hats with these apples."

"What are you going to do when you come upon these fellows?" asked the bell-boy.

"Scuttle 'em - the way they did our tent!" Tom retorted.

"I hope you pay them back generously," muttered the bell-boy. "I've a score to settle with them for trying to blacken good old Saunders! But see here! Up to date, at least, they're guests of the hotel, and I'm an employe there. Now, if they get too much the better of matters in a scrimmage, I'll sail in with you boys, even though I have to resign my hotel job. But, if I see that you can handle 'em all right, I shall just stand by without taking any part in the fight"

"We understand your position, and appreciate it," Dick replied. "We thank you, too, but we believe that we can take care of them all by ourselves. If we can't, then we'll take our drubbing."

"You boys have done some things in athletics, haven't you?" asked the bell-boy, noting the way that each of the five present members of Dick & Co. carried himself.

"Gridley High School football team last season," Dick replied, a trace of justifiable pride in his voice.

"You were?" demanded the bell-boy eagerly. "Then shake! My name is Gerard. We know a lot about the Gridley High School brand of football at Saunders."

Introductions were quickly passed.

"Now, I'd like to feel that I'm really one of you, and I'll fight shoulder to shoulder with you!" chuckled Gerard.

"Please don't try to take a hand in any fight that may occur," Prescott begged. "If you're working your way through college, just keep your eye on your job. Don't mix up in any trouble with the guests."

"We'll soon be at the spot where I left the bunch," said Gerard, a few moments later.

Over a rise of ground the bell-boy led Dick & Co. Then he pointed to a little grove of chestnut trees.

"There is the rah-rah crowd," he whispered. "You see, they have one of your lanterns, and they're lunching on some of your food supplies that they brought along with them."

"I wonder what those freshies are saying now," came in a laughing voice, from the rah-rah group under the chestnut trees.

"Their potted chicken is all right, anyway," laughed another. "Cut me off another slice of the bread. Whee! This college mischief on a dark night gives one an appetite."

Dick gave whispered instructions to his own forces, then signed to Gerard, who drew back into the shadow.

"I'd like to see the fresh kids now," jeered another rah-rah youth.

"May all your wishes in life be as promptly fulfilled!" muttered Tom Reade under his breath.

"We might have had a nice time to-night dancing with the girls from Gridley if their kid friends hadn't stepped in and spoiled it all in their juvenile way," grumbled another.

"We've finished up all the borrowed food," said another. "What shall we do next?"

"For 'next,'" roared Dick Prescott, "you fake collegians will stand up and take your medicine!"

There was instant consternation in the group under the chestnut trees. All the rah-rah boys leaped to their feet, but, ere they could stir, there was a whizzing sound on the air.

Plunk! Plunk! Ker-plunk! Missiles were flying through the air and the rah-rahs were stopping a good many of them with their own persons.

"Hey! Stop that!" bellowed one of the rah-rahs. "You - wow!"

For his utterance had been for the moment stopped by a large-sized green apple that had struck him full in the mouth.

"Hey! Let up!"

But nothing could stay the fast and furious volley of green apples until Dick & Co. had exhausted their ammunition. Most of the shots found targets, too.

Once they had had time to recover from their bewilderment the rah-rahs turned in full, inglorious flight, without attempting to strike a single blow in their own defense. Who was going to be fool enough, anyway, to run blindly into a storm of flying green apples?

Dick and his chums expended the last of their ammunition while chasing the rah-rahs. Their missiles gone, the Gridley boys put on full speed, ran after and overhauled some of their late foes and drubbed them well.

But at last, by common consent, Dick & Co. came to a halt.

"I reckon we paid the score," laughed Prescott. "They ought to let us alone hereafter."

"No doubt they will," replied Gerard grimly, coming up with the Gridley boys. "I haven't a doubt that the manager will order them to leave the hotel in the morning."

After extending their heartiest thanks to Gerard, the Gridley boys returned to their camp. There, from their supplies, they rigged new guy-ropes and erected their tent. Soon after, all hands turned in, feeling quite secure against another visitation that night.

The manager, at first, the next morning, said nothing whatever to the rah-rah youths. But, at about ten o'clock a constable appeared and gathered in all of them on a charge of disturbing the peace.

Dick & Co. were not even asked to go the justice's court. The hotel manager and bell-boy were on hand, but the crest-fallen lot of rah-rah youths all pleaded guilty. They paid fines of ten dollars apiece.

Then, on their return to the hotel, they were informed that their rooms were wanted at once.

The manager and Gerard personally escorted the rah-rah boys off the grounds of the Ashbury Terraces, and they were seen no more thereabouts. Who they were was not learned, but Gerard's word was accepted that the rah-rah boys had no connection with Saunders College.

Dick & Co. had two more pleasant meetings with their high school friends before an about-face was made, and the return hike to Gridley started.

Their liveliest adventures were yet ahead of them.

H. Irving Hancock

CHAPTER XV

MAKING PORT IN A STORM

"Did you ever see a blacker, more peculiar looking cloud coming than that one?" demanded Tom Reade, as the high school boys emerged from the gloom of a long, narrow forest road into comparatively open country.

"Is it a coming storm, or an optical delusion?" pondered Dick, halting and staring hard.

"It looks like pictures I've seen of water spouts," Greg declared.

"That's what it is," Dick replied quietly. "Though I've never seen one before, it's hard to be fooled, for that chap looks just like his published photographs. And look at that queer, brownish, half-yellowish sky back of it. It certainly looks forbidding."

"And we're going to have a stormy afternoon of it!" muttered Dave.

"The waterspout will go by to the north," Reade conjectured, studying the oddly-shaped, rapidly moving and twisting blackish cloud, "but we're going to be right in line with the main storm that is traveling with it."

"And we've got to prepare against the weather, too!" Dick cried, with sudden realization. "Fellows, the storm that is coming down on us isn't going to be any toy zephyr!"

After leaving Ashbury the boys had decided to return to Gridley by a different road.

"There's the place for us, if we can make it!" cried Dick an instant later, pointing toward the slope.

"Dave, whip up the horse. He has to travel fast for his own safety. Tom and Greg, you get behind and push the wagon up the slope. We'll all help in turn. But hustle!"

The crest of the rise of ground being made, the boys found themselves entering another forest. Dick here found the ground as favorable to his purpose as he had hoped it would be, for on the further side the land sloped downward again, and was well-wooded.

"Drive in there!" called Prescott, pointing, then ran ahead to find the best spot for pitching the tent.

"Whoa!" yelled Prescott, when he had reached the spot that he judged would do best for camp purposes. "Now, Dave, go over to the other side of the horse! Help me to get him out of the shafts. The poor animal must be our first consideration, for he can't help himself. The rest of you unload all the stuff from the wagon as fast as you can move."

Slipping the harness from the horse, Dick fastened a

halter securely, then ran the horse down into a little gully where the animal would be best protected from the force of the wind that would come with the storm.

Driving a long iron stake into the ground, Dick tethered the animal securely. Then he ran back to help his chums.

"Here's the best site for the tent," Prescott called, snatching up a stick and marking the site roughly. "Now, hustle! No; don't use the wooden stakes for the tent ropes. Drive the long iron stakes, and drive them deep!"

Then Prescott ran back with oats and corn for the horse, leaving a generous feed for the animal.

"You'll need plenty to eat, old fellow, for the storm is going to be a long and cold one."

Then Prescott ran back at full speed to his chums who were erecting the tent.

First, the four corner stakes were driven, and the guy-ropes made fast.

"Greg and Dan can drive all the other pins, if they hustle," Dick announced. "Tom, you and Dave get the floor planks down, and rig up the stove - inside the tent."

"There won't be time to lay the flooring," Reade objected, taking a hurried squint at the now more threatening sky.

"There's got to be time to lay the flooring, unless you

all want to sleep in water to-night," Dick insisted. "Harry, just break your back with the loads of wood that you bring in. I'll fill all the buckets with water."

In ten minutes more everything had been carried inside the tent. Big drops of rain were beginning to patter down.

"We've everything ready just in time to the minute," Tom Reade observed with a satisfied chuckle.

"Not everything quite ready," Prescott retorted. "Tom, if you're going to grow up to be an engineer there's one thing more you should see the need of."

"What?" challenged Reade blankly.

"Get the pick and shovel! You and I will do it. Let the rest get in under shelter!"

Standing in the rain, Tom and Dick hastily dug two ditches at either end of the tent. These ditches were no creditable engineering jobs, but they would, at need, carry a good deal of water down the slope.

By this time the rain was falling heavily. In the distance heavy thunder volleyed, and the sky was growing blacker every minute.

"One more job," called Dick. "Dave and Greg, tumble out with the shelter flap!"

This was a great sheet of canvas that had to be fastened in place over the tent roof, and at a different pitch.

"We'll be drowned before we get the shelter flap in

place," grumbled Tom.

"And we might as well be out in the rain, if we don't have it up," Dick retorted. "Open her up! Now, then - up with it!"

The shelter flap was placed with difficulty, for now the wind was driving across the country, blowing everything before it. The other two boys leaped out to help their chums. The shelter flap was made secure at last, the ropes being made fast to the surrounding trees.

By this time the wind was blowing at the rate of fifty miles an hour. The sky was nearly as black as on a dark night, while the rain was coming down "like another Niagara," as Harry Hazelton put it.

"We don't care whether we have a dry tent or not, now," laughed Dan Dalzell, as the six boys made a break for cover. "We're soaking, anyway, and a little more water won't hurt."

"I'll get a fire going in the stove," Dick smiled. "Soon after that we'll be dry enough - if the tent holds."

The stove was already in place, a sheet-iron pipe running up one of the tent walls and out through a circular opening in the canvas of the side wall opposite from the wind.

While Dick was making the fire, Tom Reade filled, trimmed and lighted the two lanterns.

"Listen to the storm!" chuckled Prescott. "But we're comfy and cheery enough. Now, peel off your outer clothes and spread them on the campstools to dry by the fire. We'll soon be feeling as cheery as though we were traveling in a Pullman car."

Within a short time all six were dry and happy. The lightning had come closer and closer, until now it flashed directly overhead, followed by heavy explosions of thunder.

Not one of the boys could remember a time when it had ever rained as hard before. It seemed to them as though solid sheets of water were coming down. Yet the position of the tent, aided by the ditches, kept their floor dry. Dan, peering out through the canvas doorway, reported that the ditches were running water at full capacity.

"This will all be over in an hour," hazarded Greg.

"It may, and it may not be," Dick rejoined. "My own guess is that the storm will last for hours."

As the howling wind gained in intensity it seemed as though the tent must be blown to ribbons, but stout canvas will stand considerable weather strain.

"If we had driven the wooden pins for the guy-ropes," muttered Greg, "everyone of them would have been washed loose by this time."

"They would have been," Dick assented, "and the tent would now be down upon our heads, a drenched wreck. As it is, I think we can pull through a night of bad weather."

In an hour the flashes of lightning had become less frequent. The wind had abated slightly, but there was no cessation of the downpour.

"I pity anyone who has to travel the highway in this storm," muttered Dave. "This isn't weather for human beings."

"Yet every bird of the air has to weather it," observed Hazelton.

"Yes," muttered Tom, "and a good many of the birds of the air will be killed in this storm, too."

Night came down early. The wind and rain had sent the temperature down until it seemed to the high school boys more like an October night. The warmth and light in the tent were highly gratifying to all.

"As long as the tent holds I can't think of a blessed thing we have to go outside for," sighed Reade contentedly.

"We don't have to," laughed Dick. "Fellows, we're away off in the wilderness, but we're as happy as we could be in a palace. How about supper?"

That idea was approved instantly.

"We'll have two suppers to-night," proposed Tom. "That will be the visible proof and expression of the highest happiness that can be reached on a night like this."

Even by ten o'clock that night there was no abatement in the volume of rain falling. The wind still howled.

"Are we going to turn in, soon?" inquired Dave.

"My vote," announced Tom indolently, "is for another supper, and turn in at perhaps two o'clock in the morning."

"I second the motion - -as far as another supper goes," chimed in Danny Grin.

"It wants to be a supper of piping hot stuff, too," declared Greg. "It's warm here in the tent, but the surrounding world is chill and drear. Nothing but hot food will serve us."

Preparations for the meal were quickly under way.

"I hope everyone within the reach of this storm is as comfortable as we are," murmured Hazelton.

"Why, we're so happy, we could entertain company with a relish," laughed Reade.

"Say, what was that?" demanded Greg.

From outside came a faint sound as of someone stealthily groping about outside in the storm.

"Bring a lantern, quickly!" called Dick, going toward the tent door.

As Greg played the rays of light against the darkness outside, Dick suddenly sprang forth into the dark. Then he returned, bearing in his arms the pitiful little figure of old Reuben Hinman, the peddler.

"Look at his head!" gasped Reade, in horror, as Prescott entered with the burden.

From a gash over the peddler's left temple blood was flowing, leaving its dark trail over the peddler's light brown coat.

Dick carried the stricken old man straight to his own cot, laying him there gently.

"Who can have done this deed?" gasped Greg, throbbing with sympathy for the poor old man.

Outside other approaching steps sounded. Dave and Tom, snatching up sticks of firewood, sprang forward.

CHAPTER XVI

HOME, HOSPITAL AND ALMSHOUSE

Greg flashed the lantern on four hulking, bedraggled ragged men.

"Hello! It's the same kids!" cried a hoarse voice out in the storm. "They'll be glad to see us."

"You keep out of here!" ordered Reade, thrusting his stick at the face of the first tramp - the boss tramp - who tried to enter.

"No!" countermanded Dick Prescott. "Let even the hoboes come in. Let anyone come in on a night like this."

"Now, that's decent of you," admitted the boss tramp, as he sloshed heavily in, followed by three companions. Two of these tramps had been with the "boss" on another well remembered occasion. The third was a stranger to Dick & Co.

"My, but you've got a real house in here a true port in a storm," observed the boss tramp, as he halted to stare about him. "Friends, this is the best thing we've seen today."

H. Irving Hancock

"It is," agreed the other tramps solemnly.

The glance of the newcomers did not rest upon the face of Reuben Hinman, for Prescott had gently spread a blanket so that it effectually concealed the little old peddler.

"What have you men been doing?" asked Dick, straightening up and eyeing them coldly, steadily.

"Drowning in the woods," replied the boss, "for we knew we couldn't find a house or barn within two miles, and the road is like a river you need a boat for travel to-night. When the storm came we men made a brush lean-to and kept as dry as we could under it. But it got worse and worse. But at last we caught sight of your light shining through the trees. So we headed for it. We hoped you'd have a stove with a fire in it, and you have - so we're all right, and much obliged."

"Keep back there a bit," ordered Dick, so firmly that the tramps obeyed. "Dave, help me to lift this cot over within a few feet of the stove. Be as gentle as you can."

Four tramps looked on in solemn curiosity as they saw Darrin and Prescott lift a cot on which lay something completely covered by a blanket.

Then Dick turned down the blanket, revealing the bruised, bleeding head of Reuben Hinman.

"What do you men know about this?" Prescott demanded, eyeing them compellingly.

But the tramps' look was one of such astonished innocence that Prescott began to wonder whether he had wrongly suspected these knights of the highway.

"Why did you do - this?" Prescott sternly insisted.

"We - we didn't do it!" exclaimed the boss tramp fervently. "We didn't even know that this old party was anywhere out in the storm. We -"

Moaning, Reuben Hinman stirred slightly then opened his eyes dreamily.

"Mr. Hinman, can you talk?" asked Dick gently.

"Ye-es," faintly admitted the peddler.

"Then how were you hurt, sir?" Dick pressed in the same gentle voice.

"I - I saw the light. Tried - to drive my horse - in. Wagon turned over. Fell off - and hurt my head," replied the peddler, whispering hoarsely.

"You're fully conscious, Mr. Hinman, and know just what you're saying?" Dick pressed.

"Yes, Prescott. I know."

"Then no one else assaulted you to-night, sir."

"No - one."

"I feel like saying 'thank heaven' for that!" exclaimed Dick in a quiet voice, as he straightened up, his eyes a trifle misty. "I hate to think that the earth holds men vile enough to strike down a weak old man like this!"

"And on such a night," added Tom Reade.

"Oh, we're pretty bad," said the boss tramp, huskily, "but we didn't do anything like that."

"At first," Dick went on, "I thought you hoboes had done the deed. That was why I asked my friend to let you come in. I wanted to keep you here until we could find someone who would take care of you."

"We didn't do it," replied the boss tramp, "and the old man says we didn't."

"No; no man struck me - I fell," chimed in the peddler weakly.

"We'll help you take care of the old man," offered the boss tramp.

"If you mean what you say," Prescott proposed, "then take one of these lanterns and go down by the road to see what you can find out about Mr. Hinman's horse and wagon. Or did you see them as you came up?"

"No, for we came through the woods," replied the boss tramp. "I'll take the lantern. Come with me, Joe."

Out into the dark plunged the two tramps, to face the heavily falling rain. For once, at any rate, they were doing something useful.

At a signal from Dick, Greg put some water on the stove to heat. Prescott found some clean cloth in their wardrobe box and bathed the wound on Mr. Hinman's temple, then washed his entire face. The wound proved to be broad, rather than deep, and was such as might have been caused by falling on sharp pebbles. Then Dick bound up the wound.

Next, Dick and Greg undressed Mr. Hinman and rubbed him down, then rolled him in dry blankets and laid him on another cot not far from the stove.

"Come out, you other hoboes," called the boss tramp's voice. "Come and help us right the peddler's wagon and bring that and the horse up here."

The other two tramps went reluctantly out into the storm.

A bottle full of hot water, wrapped in a towel, was placed at the peddler's feet.

In the meantime the tramps got the wagon into a sheltered position, then staked the horse out close to the place where the Gridley horse was tethered. This having been accomplished, they came back to the camp, to find a new aroma on the air.

"That stuff smells good. What is it?" asked the boss tramp.

"Ginger tea. We've made some to give to Mr. Hinman."

"Will you give us some, too?" asked the tramp. "We're all of us chilled and hoarse."

"I will," Dick nodded, "if you men will undertake to fill the buckets before you try to dry yourselves. Otherwise, we shall run out of water."

Grunting, the boss tramp and one of his companions listened while Dick directed them where to find running water. Out again into the storm they lurched, and soon had all the water buckets filled and in the tent.

While the tramps dried their clothing, Prescott kept his word about making ginger tea.

"This seems like the best stuff I've had since I was a baby," remarked the boss tramp, in a somewhat grateful voice.

"Maybe that's because you've worked for it," suggested Reade thoughtfully.

"I wonder," grunted the hobo. "I wonder."

Later on Dick and his chums prepared a supper, of which all partook except the peddler, who needed sleep and warmth more.

The tramps slept on the floor, later on. Tom, Dave and Harry slept on their cots, while the other three high school boys remained awake.

Toward two o'clock in the morning Dick found Reuben Hinman's skin becoming decidedly feverish, and began to administer nitre.

"I'd mount our horse, and try to ride for a doctor, if I thought I could get one," murmured Greg.

"You couldn't get one here to-night," volunteered the boss tramp, who had awakened and had risen on one elbow. "Neither an automobile nor a buggy could be driven over this wild road to-night. The water is three feet deep in spots - worse in some others."

Though the deluge outside still continued, all would have been cheery inside had it not been for the alarm Dick & Co. felt over the increasing fever of the poor old peddler. His breathing became more and more labored.

Dave awoke and came over to listen and look on.

"I'll try to go for a doctor," he whispered.

"You might even reach one," Dick replied. "I'd be willing to try myself, but we couldn't get a physician through on a night like this."

"At least I'll go down and have a look at the road," muttered Reade, rising, wrapping himself up as best he could, and taking a lantern.

Tom presently returned, looking like a drowned rat.

"It's no go," he announced gloomily. "The road is a river."

"Sure it is," muttered the boss tramp, "or - as you lads have been so decent to me - I'd go myself and try to find a doctor."

CHAPTER XVII

TWO KINDS OF HOBO

Toward daylight the rain ceased. Dawn came in heavy and misty, but after an hour the sun shone forth, dispelling the low-lying clouds.

Dick was sound asleep at this time, Tom and Harry having relieved the other watchers. All of the tramps lay stretched on the hard wooden floor, since none of the high school boys cared to have one of these fellows lying on his cot even when it was not in use.

"Go down and take a look at the road, Hazy," Tom desired, after the sun had been out for an hour.

"The water's running out of the road, or drying off, pretty fast" Hazelton reported on his return. "Still, a doctor would have a hard job getting over the road as yet."

"Did you see anyone trying to get over the road with a vehicle?" Reade inquired.

"Not a soul or a wheel," Harry answered. "As far as travel goes the road might as well be a strip of the Sahara Desert."

Reuben Hinman's breathing was so labored that it disturbed the watchers a good deal.

"We're doing all we can for you, and we'll get better care for you, just as soon as we can," Tom explained, resting a hand on the fever-flushed face.

"I know," wheezed the old man painfully. "Good boy!"

By eight o'clock all hands were astir.

"Are we going to get any breakfast to-day?" asked the tramp known as Joe.

"Yes," nodded Dick, choking back the temptation to say something caustic.

By nine o'clock the meal had been eaten. The stove now made the tent so hot that Mr. Hinman's cot had to be moved to the farther end and the tent flaps thrown open to admit cooler air.

Greg had attended to feeding both of the horses, which had gotten through the dismal night without very much discomfort.

Now Dick went down to look at the road.

"I'm going to mount our horse, bareback, and keep straight on up the road," he announced, coming back. "I will not have to go very far before I find a physician."

"No, you're not going, either," broke in the boss tramp. "I am going."

"But, see here, I can't very well let a stranger like you go off with our horse," Dick objected smilingly.

"You don't have to," retorted the other. "I'll go on foot, and I'll make the trip as fast as I can, too. But maybe you'd better give me a note to the doctor. He might not pay much attention to a sick call from a fellow who looks as tough as I do."

"If I let you go, can I depend upon you to keep right on going straight and fast, until you deliver a note to a doctor?" asked Prescott, eyeing the boss tramp keenly.

"Yes!" answered the tramp, returning the glance with one so straightforward that Dick felt he could really trust the man. "And if the first doctor won't or can't come, I'll keep on going until I find one who will take the call."

"Good for you!" cried Tom Reade heartily. "And if it weren't for fear of startling you, I'd say that the next thing you'll be doing will be to find and accept a job, and work again like a useful man!"

"That would be startling," grinned the fellow, half sullenly.

Dick wrote the note. Away went his ill-favored looking messenger. Dick turned to administer more nitre to the peddler.

"Do you expect to move on at all to-day?" Dave asked of Dick.

"It wouldn't be really wise, would it?" Dick counter-queried. "Our tent and shelter flap are pretty wet to take down and fold away in a wagon. We'd find it wet going, too. Hadn't we better stay here until to-morrow, and then break camp with our tent properly dry?"

All hands voted in favor of remaining - except the hoboes, who weren't asked. They would remain indefinitely, anyway, if permitted, and if the food held out.

But Dick soon set them to work. One was despatched for water, the other two set to gathering wet firewood and spreading it in the sun to dry out. Nor did the trio of remaining tramps refuse to do the work required of them, though they looked reluctant enough at first.

Two more hours passed.

"I'm afraid our friend, Hustling Weary, is having a hard time to get a doctor who'll come down the road," Dick remarked to Darrin.

"Oh, the doctor will come, if Weary has found him," Dave replied. "Doctors always come. They have to, or lose their reputations."

Half an hour later a business-like honk! was heard. Then, through the trees Dick & Co. saw an automobile halt down at the side of the road. A tall, stout man, who looked to be about sixty-five years old, but who displayed the strength and speed of a young man, leaped from the car, followed by the tramp messenger.

"Mr. Prescott?" called the big stranger.

"Yes, sir," bowed Dick.

"Dr. Hewitt. Let me see your patient."

For some minutes the physician bent over the peddler, examining and questioning the old man, who answered with effort.

"I must get Hinman to a hospital some miles from here," the physician explained, aside, to Dick. "The poor old man is going to have pneumonia, and he'd die without hospital care. Probably he'll die, anyway. I'll give him a hypodermic injection in the arm, then wait for him to become quiet. After that we'll move him to the tonneau of my car and I'll take him to the hospital. I telephoned Hinman's son, over at Fenton, telling him where his father and his wagon are. The son ought to come over and take charge of the outfit."

It was three quarters of an hour later when Dr. Hewitt examined his patient, then remarked:

"He can be moved now, as well as at any time."

"There's someone coming," announced Reade, as the sound of a horse's hoofs were heard. Tom went out to look at the new arrival.

A man of forty, rather flashily dressed, though somewhat mud-spattered, rode up on a horse that looked much the worse for being abroad on the bad roads.

"I understand that Mr. Hinman is here, ill," began the stranger.

"He is," Tom nodded. "Have you any interest in him?"

"Mr. Hinman is my father."

"Come right in," Tom invited, throwing open the flap of the tent.

"Hold my horse, will you?"

Something in the younger Hinman's way of making the request caused Reade's backbone to stiffen.

"I see that you have a piece of halter rope," Tom replied. "You may tie your horse to any one of the trees. They don't belong to me."

The son frowned, but led his mount to a tree, hitching it there. Then he turned and entered the tent.

"How are you, father?" asked the younger Hinman, crossing to the cot and bending over the old man.

"Better, already, I think," replied Reuben Hinman feebly.

"I should hope so," replied Timothy Hinman, looking more than a trifle annoyed. "You had no business to be out in that storm."

"I couldn't help -" began the old man slowly, but Dr. Hewitt broke in almost fiercely:

"Your father is in no condition to talk, Mr. Hinman. I telephoned you so that you might come over and take charge of the horse and wagon. There is quite a bit of stock on the wagon, too, I believe."

"My father must have considerable money with him," the young man hinted.

"He has some," Dick replied. "I do not know how much."

"I will take charge of his money for him," offered young Hinman.

"You will do nothing of the sort," broke in Dr. Hewitt, scowling. "Hinman, your father will be some time at the hospital, and he will want to be able to pay his bills there. He will also want to be able to purchase some comforts for himself while convalescing. So your father will take his money with him to the hospital."

"He can turn it over to me, if he has a mind to do so," insisted the younger man.

"You get out of here!" ordered the doctor, speaking decisively, though in a low tone. At the same time he pointed to the doorway of the tent. Just then the doctor looked as though he might rather enjoy the opportunity of throwing young Hinman out into the open air. The peddler's son walked outside of the tent with an air of offended dignity.

"Now, will four of you young men take hold of that cot, gently, and carry it out to my car?" asked Dr. Hewitt.

Dick, Dave, Tom and Greg served as the litter bearers. Then, under Dr. Hewitt's instructions, they lifted the old man into the tonneau of the car as though he had been an infant. The boss tramp had already taken his place in the tonneau of the machine. After blankets brought by the physician had been wrapped about the peddler the tramp contrived to rest the old man against his own broad shoulder.

"Good-bye, father," said the younger Hinman, who had looked on with a frown on his face. "I hope you'll be all right soon."

Reuben Hinman tried to smile. He also moved as though trying to stretch out a hand to his son, but the folds of the blankets prevented.

Dr. Hewitt went back to the tent to get his medicine case, which he had intentionally left behind. As he went he signed to Dick & Co. to accompany him.

"You young men haven't done anything for the old man for which I am going to commend you," said the physician bluntly. "You've simply done what any upright, humane, decent people would have done for a stricken old man, and you've done it well. But by contrast you noticed the younger Hinman's conduct. He is not worried that his father is ill, but hopes that the old man will soon be back at his work. Of course, he hopes that his father will be at work, soon; for when the old man stops working the younger man will very likely have to go to work himself."

"You don't mean, doctor, that that big, healthy-looking fellow is supported by his father?" gasped Dick Prescott.

"That's just what I mean," nodded the man of medicine.

"Why, I didn't suppose that old Mr. Hinman earned much."

"In the tin-peddler's business it's nearly all profit except the wear and tear on horse and wagon," smiled the physician. "One who isn't fitted for that line of work would starve to death at it, but Reuben Hinman has always been a shrewd, keen dealer in his own line of work. Strange as it may seem, Reuben is believed to make more than three hundred dollars a month. He gives it all to that son and two daughters. He wanted to bring his children up to be ladies and gentlemen - and they are! They are all three of them too shiftless to do any work. They take the old man's money, but they won't live with him. They are too busy in 'society' to bother with the old man. On what he is able to turn over to his children every month they keep a rather pretentious home in Fenton, though they live a full mile away from their father. They never go near him, except for more money. If they meet him on his wagon, or when he is walking in his old clothes, they refuse to recognize him. Yet, though Reuben Hinman isn't a fool in anything else, he is very proud of the fact that his son is a 'gentleman,' and that his daughters are 'ladies.' Now, in a nutshell, you know the tragedy of the old man's life. Young Tim Hinman would, if he could, take the old man's money away from him at once and let him go to the hospital as a charity patient."

"Humph!" muttered Dick, and then was silent.

Timothy Hinman, when Dr. Hewitt and the boys stepped outside the tent, was inspecting the dingy old red wagon with a look of contempt on his face.

"What am I going to do with this crazy old rattle-trap?" inquired young Hinman plaintively. "Would one of you boys accept a dollar to drive this over to Fenton, and put the horse up in my father's barn? The trip can be made in two days of good driving."

Dick Prescott shook his head in order that he might avoid speaking.

"I came by train, within five miles of here, then hired a horse and rode over here," the younger Hinman went on. "So I've got to take the horse back to where I got it, and then return by train. So I'll pay a dollar and a half to the boy who will drive this rig back to Fenton."

This time there was no response to the magnificent offer.

"See here," muttered young Hinman half savagely, "it's more than the job is worth, but I'll pay two dollars to have this rig driven home. Will you take the job?"

He looked directly at Dick Prescott, who replied bluntly:

"Thank you; I won't."

"But what on earth am I going to do with the horse and wagon, then?" demanded Timothy Hinman, as though he found Prescott's refusal preposterous.

"I would suggest," offered Dick coolly, "that you drive your father's rig home yourself."

"I drive it?" gasped the son.

"Certainly."

"But it's no job for a gentleman!" protested the younger Mr. Hinman, looking very much aghast.

"Then I don't know whether or not the owner of these

woods would consent to your leaving your father's property here," replied Prescott, as he turned on his heel.

Dr. Hewitt had watched the scene with a good deal of amusement. Now the physician turned to see whether his patient were as comfortable as possible.

"My man," said the doctor, to the boss tramp, "you hold my patient as comfortably and skillfully as though you had once been a nurse. Were you ever one?"

"No, sir," replied the tramp. "It just comes natural."

"I've been looking for a man to work for me," continued Dr. Hewitt, regarding the tramp with calculating eyes. "I believe that you've got in you the making of a real man if you'd only stop being a tramp. How would you like to try it out?"

"I dunno," replied the boss tramp, looking a bit staggered.

"If you go to work for me, I don't want you to take it up as a casual experiment," went on the man of medicine. "I haven't any time for experiments. But, if you'll declare positively that you're going to make a useful man of yourself, and that you'll live up to what I expect of you, I'll take you on. I won't have an idler about my place, and I won't tolerate any use of alcohol. If you shirk or drink - even once out you go. But I'll start you at ten dollars a month and board, and raise you - if I keep you - two dollars a month until you're getting thirty dollars a month and board as a steady thing. Are you man enough to take me up, and to make it worth my while to take you on?"

"Yes," replied the boss tramp huskily, after a struggle with himself.

"All right, then, we'll see how much a man you are. By the way, what's your name?"

"Jim Joggers," replied the tramp.

Dr. Hewitt eyed the fellow keenly for a few seconds, before he replied, with a slight smile:

"All right; we'll let it go at Joggers until you've put yourself far enough forward so that you'll be willing to use your own name."

Honk! honk! The car was under way.

When Dick and his three friends turned back to the tent they found all three of the remaining tramps in there, smoking vile pipes and playing with a greasy, battered pack of cards. "The weather's fine again," announced Dick, "and you'll find us the most hospitable fellows you ever met. My friends, we take pleasure in offering you the whole outside world in which to play!"

"Talk United States!" growled one of the tramps, without looking up from the game.

"Tom," laughed Prescott, turning to Reade, "strange dialects are your specialty. Kindly translate, into 'United States,' what I have just said to these men."

"I will," agreed Tom. "Attention, hoboes! Look right at me! That's right. Now - git!"

"You might let us stay on a bit longer," grumbled one

of the tramps. "We ain't bothering you folks any."

"Only eating us out of house and home," snapped Dave.

"And delaying the time when we must wash up the tent after you," added Danny Grin.

But the tramps played on, smoked on.

"Did you fellows ever hear of that famous man, Mr. A. Quick Expediter?" Tom asked the tramps.

"No," growled one of them.

"Expediter was a truly great man," Tom continued. "He had a motto. It was a short one. One word, and that word was - 'git'!"

"We are famed for our courtesy," remarked Darry. "We'd hate to lose even a shred of our reputation in that line. But in these present years of our young lives we are football players by training, and high school boys merely for pleasure. We know some of the dandiest tackles you ever saw. Shall we show you a few of them? If you object to observing our tackles - and sharing in the effects - then signify your wishes by placing yourselves at a safe distance from such enthusiastic football wranglers as we are."

Greg, Danny Grin and Harry were already crouching as though for a spring. Dave took his place in an imaginary football line-up, leaning slightly forward. Tom Reade sighed, then advanced to the line. All were waiting for the battle signal from Dick Prescott.

By this time the most talkative of the three tramps noted the signs of a gathering squall.

"Come on, mates," he urged, with a sulky growl, "let's get out of here. These young fellows want their place all to themselves. They're just like all of the capitalistic class that are ruining the country to-day! Things in this country are coming to a pass where there's nothing for the fellow who -"

"Who won't work hard enough to get the place in the world that he wants," Tom Reade finished for the tramp, as he ushered the three of them through the doorway.

H. Irving Hancock

CHAPTER XVIII

DICK PRESCOTT, KNIGHT ERRANT

That day of enforced tie-up was followed by three days of hard hiking. The Gridley High School boys showed the fine effects of their two vigorous, strenuous outings. Each had taken on weight slightly, though there was no superfluous flesh on any of the six. They were bronzed, comparatively lean-looking, trim and hard. Their muscles were at the finest degree of excellence.

"We set out to get ourselves as hard as nails," remarked Dave, as the boys bathed in a secluded bit of woodland through which a creek flowed. It was, the morning of their fourth day of renewed hiking. After the swim and breakfast that was to follow, there were twenty miles of rural roads to be covered before the evening camp was pitched.

"I guess we've won all we set out to get, haven't we?" inquired Reade, squaring his broad shoulders with an air of pride. "I feel equal to anything that a fellow of my size and years could do."

"I think, without boasting, we may consider ourselves the six most valuable candidates for Gridley High School football this year," Prescott declared. "We ought to be the best men for the team; we've worked hard to get ourselves in the pink of physical condition."

"I wouldn't care to be any stronger than I am," laughed Danny Grin. "If I were any stronger folks would be saying that I ought to go to work."

"You will have to go to work within another year," Dick laughed, "whatever that work may be. But you must work with your brain, Danny boy, if you're to get any real place in life. Your muscles are intended only as a sign that your body is going to be equal to all the demands that your brain may make on that body."

"If my mental ability were equal to my physical strength I wouldn't have to work at all," grinned Dalzell.

Splash! His dive carried him under the surface of the water. Presently he came up, blowing, then swimming with strong strokes.

"Danny boy seems to have the same idea so many people have," laughed Prescott. "They think that a man who does all his real work with his brain isn't working at all, just because he doesn't get into a perspiration and wilt his collar."

Splash! splash! Reade and Darrin were in the water racing upstream.

"I don't know when I've ever found so much happiness in a summer," asserted Greg, as he poised himself for a dive into the water.

"I wonder if Timmy Hinman ever had the nerve to

stick to his father's wagon long enough to get it back to Fenton," said Dave, as he swam beside Reade.

"If he ever took that wagon home, I'll wager that he drove the last few miles late at night, so that his 'society' friends wouldn't have the shock of seeing him drive the peddling outfit that sustains him," Reade replied.

"I'll never forget the younger Hinman's disgusted look when he tried to drive the outfit from our camp, the other morning, with his saddle mount tied behind and balking on the halter," grinned Darry.

"I wonder why such fellows as Timothy Hinman were ever created," Tom went on. "Every time I think about the gentlemanly Timmy I feel as though I wanted to kick something."

Only the day before, stopping at a postoffice on the route, as had been arranged with Dr. Hewitt, Dick & Co. had received word that the peddler was seriously ill with pneumonia, with all the chances against his recovery.

"If the peddler should die," suggested Dave soberly, "do you believe that Timmy Hinman will be able to face the thought of going to work for a living?"

"It would be an awful fate," Tom declared grimly. "Timmy might try to work, but I don't know whether he would be able to live through the shock and shame of having to earn the money for paying his own bills in life."

"There's that irrepressible Dick again!" called Greg

five minutes later.

"What's he up to now?" asked Tom, from further up the creek.

"He has had his rub-down, got his clothing on and is now at work frying bacon and eggs."

"Then don't disturb him," begged Reade, "or he might fry short of the quantity of food that is really going to be required."

Five minutes more, however, saw the last of the boys out of water and rapidly getting themselves in shape to perform their own required duties. There could be no idlers in the party when Dick & Co. were away from home on a hike.

Yet, once breakfast had been disposed of, and the dishes washed, there seemed something in the August air that made them all disinclined to break camp and move on.

"I wish we could stay here all day, and move on to-morrow," murmured Hazy, thus voicing the thought of some of the others.

"And then blame the tramps for loafing!" exclaimed Dick.

"Do we look as though we had loafed this summer?" challenged Dalzell.

"No; but one or two of you would have done a good deal of it if you hadn't been afraid of the contempt of the others," smiled Prescott.

"Honestly, now," demanded Hazy, "wouldn't you enjoy just staying here and lounging today, Dick Prescott?"

"I would," Dick assented.

"There, now!"

"But that isn't what we left home to do, so we won't do it."

"Eh?" queried Hazy.

"Attention, Lazybones Squad!" called Prescott, springing up. "Hazy, harness the horse and hitch him to the wagon. Tom, Dave and Greg, take down the tent. I'll pack the bedding. Dan, load the kitchen stuff on the wagon."

This occupied a few minutes.

"Now, all hands turn to and load on the floor planks, bedding and the tent," called Dick.

This, too, was quickly accomplished, though all six were now perspiring.

"Greg, I believe it's your turn to drive first to-day," Prescott announced. "Up with you! Forward - march!"

Dick led the way out of camp, at a brisk four-mile-an-hour stride. The long hike was started, at last. After that there was no grumbling, even during the hourly halt of ten minutes.

The noon halt found them with eleven and a half miles

covered out of the twenty. Five o'clock brought Dick & Co. to the outskirts of Fenton, a town of some twenty-five hundred inhabitants.

"Whoa!" called Tom, reining up half a mile from the town. "There are woods here, Dick. If we go any closer to Fenton, we'll either have to keep on traveling to the other side of the town, or ask the authorities for permission to camp on the common. Don't you believe we had better stop here?"

"These are the woods that Dave and I had just picked out," Prescott replied. "We were going to keep on traveling until we found out who owns the woods. This isn't quite in the wilderness, Tom, and we must begin again to seek permission to make our camp from owners of property."

"If these are the woods," grunted Tom, "there can be no use in going farther. You and Dave trot on ahead, and bring us back word."

"All right," sang out the young leader, "but don't drive onto the ground, or unpack, until we are back with word about the owner's permission."

Three minutes of walking brought them to a farmhouse that looked like the abode of prosperous people.

"Well, what is it?" demanded a stout man, with a good-humored face, as he stepped out from a barn.

"We wish to know, sir," Dick explained, "if you can tell us who owns the woods about a quarter of a mile back, at the right hand side of the road?"

"I think I can," nodded the man. "Will you describe the woods a little more particularly?"

As Prescott complied the farmer broke in:

"Those are my woods, all right. What do you want of them?"

Dick explained the desire of himself and his friends to camp there for the night.

"Who are you boys?" asked the farmer, keenly eyeing Dick and Dave.

"Gridley High School boys, out on a vacation jaunt."

"You won't do any damage to my woods, will you?"

"Certainly not, sir," Dick promised.

"Then go right ahead and pitch your camp, young man. Enjoy yourselves."

"We shall have to gather and use quite a bit of firewood, sir," Prescott continued.

"Well, there's considerable dead wood lying about there."

"May we pay you a proper price for the use of the firewood, sir?" Prescott went on.

"If you try to," laughed the farmer, "I'll chase you out of the woods. Make yourselves at home, boys. Have as good a time as you can."

"Thank you, sir."

"And - have you had any fresh milk lately?"

"Not a lot of it, sir."

"Would you like some?"

"Why, if we may pay -"

"You may pay me," promptly agreed the farmer, "by bringing the pail back when you pass this way in the morning."

With that remark he went into another building, soon coming out with an eight-quart pail filled with milk.

"This sort of stuff isn't much good, except when you haven't had any for a long time," laughed the farmer. "Enjoy yourselves. Say, you don't play football with the Gridley High School eleven, do you?"

"All of us do," Dick admitted.

"Thought so," chuckled the farmer. "That's why I was interested in you. I saw the Thanksgiving game at Gridley last year. Great game nervy lot of boys, with all their sand about them. There was one fellow in particular, I remember, who broke doctor's orders and jumped into the game at the last minute. He saved the game for Gridley, I heard. I'd like to shake hands with him."

"Then here's your chance, sir," laughed Dave, shoving Dick forward. "Mr. Dick Prescott, Gridley High School."

"My name's Dobbins," smiled the farmer, extending his hand. "Glad to meet you, Prescott. I thought it was you all the time. Mebbe the young man with you is Darrin."

"Yes," laughed Dick, and there was more handshaking.

"I hope I'll see the rest of your friends when you pass in the morning," said the farmer cordially.

"Hiram - supper!" called a shrill voice from The doorway.

"Coming, mother! Boys, it does one good to meet the right sort of fellows once in a while. Enjoy the woods in your own way, won't you?"

"That man is right. As he says, it does one good to meet the right sort of fellow once in a while - and he's the right sort," declared Darry fervently, as the chums trudged back to their outfit.

Camp was pitched, and supper was soon under way. When it was all over, and everything cleaned up, Dick looked about him at his friends.

"I wonder if any of you fellows feel the way I do to-night?" he asked. "We still have our white clothes, and Fenton is something of a town. We've been in the woods for so long that I feel just like dressing up in white and taking a stroll into town."

Tom, Dan and Dave voted in the affirmative. Greg and Hazy averred that they had walked enough for one day. So the four boys donned white, while the other two remained behind in flannel and khaki.

Dick and the three companions of his stroll when almost in Fenton, were passing through a street of pretty little cottages when a tiny figure, clad in white ran out of the darkness, bumping into Dick's knees.

"Hello, little one!" cried Prescott, cheerily, picking up a wee little girl of four and holding her at arm's length. "Hello, you're crying. What's the matter? Lost mother?"

"No; lost papa," wailed the little one.

"Perhaps we can find him for you," offered Tom, readily.

"Mollie! Mollie, where are you?" came a woman's voice out of the darkness.

"Is this your little girl, madam?" called Prescott. "We'll bring her to you."

In another moment the woman, young and pretty, also dressed in white, had reached the child and was holding her by the hand.

"Oh, you little runaway!" chided Dave, smilingly, as he bent over, wagging a finger at the child.

"No; it's papa that runned away," gasped the little one, in a frightened voice. "He ran away to a saloon."

"Oh, said Dave, straightening up and feeling embarrassed as he caught the humiliated look in the young woman's face.

"Pa - runned away and made mama cry," the little one

babbled on, half sobbing. "I must go after him and bring him home."

"Be quiet, Mollie," commanded her mother.

"Papa comes, if he knows you want him," insisted the child. "I tell him you want him - that you cry because he went to saloon."

For an instant the mother caught her breath. Then she began to cry bitterly. Dick and his friends wished themselves almost anywhere else.

"It's too bad when the children get old enough to realize it," said the woman, brokenly. Then, of a sudden, she eyed Dick and his chums bravely.

"Boys," she said, "I hope the time will never come when you'll feel that it's manly to go out with the crowd and spend the evening in drinking."

"The way we feel about it now," spoke Dick, sympathetically, "we'd rather be dead than facing any degradation of the sort."

They were only boys, and they were strangers to the woman. Moreover, little Mollie was looking pleadingly towards Dick, as if loath to let him go. In her misery the young wife poured out her story to her sympathetic listeners. Her husband had been a fine young fellow - was still young. His drinking had begun only three months before.

"We have our own home, more than half paid for," added the woman, pointing to a pretty little cottage. "Tom has always been a good workman, never out of a job. But lately he has been spending his wages for drink. Last month we didn't make our payment on the house. Today he got his month's pay, and promised not to drink any more. He was going to take us into town to-night for a good time, and we were happy, weren't we, baby? Then two of his saloon cronies passed the house. Tom went with them, but said he would come right back for us. He hasn't come yet, and he won't come now until midnight. The month's pay will be gone, and that means that the home will be gone, after a little. Boys, I shall never see you again, and it has seemed a help to me to talk to you. Remember, don't ever -"

"Madam," asked Dick, suddenly, in a husky tone, "do you mind telling us your husband's name, and the name of the place where he has gone?"

"His name is Tom Drake, and he has gone up to Miller's place," answered Mrs. Drake. "But why do you ask? What -"

"Mrs. Drake," Dick continued, earnestly, "we don't want to be meddlers, and we'll keep out of this, if you request it. But the child has given me an inspiration that I could help you. If you authorize me, I'll go to Miller's and see if I can't help your husband to know that his happiness is right here, not in a saloon."

"I - I fear that will be a big undertaking," quivered Mrs. Drake.

A big undertaking, indeed, it was bound to be!

CHAPTER XIX

"I'LL FIGHT HIM FOR THIS MAN!"

"It's wonderfully kind of you!" breathed the woman, gratefully. "But it really won't do any good. When a man has begun to drink nothing can reclaim him from it. My only hope is to be able to have a talk with Tom when his money is gone."

"Of course if you dislike to have us try, Mrs. Drake -" Dick began.

"I don't dislike to have you try!" cried the woman, quickly. "All I am thinking about is the hopelessness of your undertaking. You simply can't get Tom out of Miller's to-night until the owner of that awful place turns him out at closing time. I know! This has happened before."

Dick stood in an uncertain attitude, his cap in hand. The appealing face of the child, looking eagerly up at him, made him wish with all his heart to try to do a good act here, yet he couldn't think of going on such an errand without the young wife's permission.

"Let him go, mama," urged the child. "He'll bring papa back."

Dick looked questioningly at the woman.

"All right, then, go," she acquiesced. "Oh, I hope you have good luck, and that you don't make Tom ugly, either. I'll say, for him, that he has never been ugly yet."

"Mrs. Drake, we all four accept your commission - or permission, whichever it is," replied Dick, bowing. "We'll try to use tact and judgment, and we'll try to bring Mr. Drake back with us."

Dick asked a few questions as to where Miller's place might be found. Then he set off, he and his chums walking abreast.

"Bring him back!" Mollie said plaintively. "Then mama won't cry, and I won't, either."

"I feel like a fool!" muttered Tom Reade, when they were out of earshot of the waiting mother and child.

"If you don't like the undertaking, you might keep in the background," Dick suggested.

"It's likely I'd back out of anything that's moving, isn't it?" Reade demanded, offended. "I don't mind any disagreeable business that we may run into. But I feel like a fool when I think of the message we'll have to take back to that poor woman and baby."

"Tom Drake will deliver the message to them," replied Dick, firmly.

"If he's sober even now," murmured Danny Grin, uneasily.

"I'm strong for the task!" declared Dave Darrin, with enthusiasm.

"So would I be," Tom defended himself, "if I thought that even a night of fighting would result in anything like success. But -"

"Better stop right here, then," Prescott, suggested, smiling earnestly. But neither of Dick's companions stopped.

They were walking briskly, now. As they had been told, Miller's was the first place on the right hand side, where the business street of Fenton began. It had been a tavern in the old days, and was still a big and roomy structure.

Yet there was no mistaking the room in which the object of their quest was to be found. The door of the saloon opened repeatedly while the boys stood regarding the place.

Dick stepped over to a man who had just come out.

"Is Tom Drake in there?" Dick asked.

"Yes."

"Is he sober?" Dick pressed.

"Yes; so far," answered the man.

"Will you do me a great favor? Just step inside and tell him that there is a man outside who wants to see him. Just tell him that, and nothing more."

"Are you from Drake's wife?" asked the man, looking Dick over shrewdly.

"Yes," Dick admitted, candidly.

"I'll do it," nodded the man. "Drake has been making a fool of himself. He'll go to pieces and find himself without a job before the year is out. You wait here. I'll find a way to coax him out for you."

Soon the door opened again, and there came out Prescott's messenger followed by a clean-cut, well-built young man of not more than twenty-eight years of age.

"There's the young man who says he wants to see you," the citizen explained, pointing to Dick.

Tom Drake walked steadily enough. He certainly was not yet much under the influence of liquor.

"You wanted to see me?" he asked, looking somewhat puzzled as he eyed young Prescott.

"Yes," Dick admitted.

"What about?"

"Will you take a short walk with me," Dick went on, "and I'll explain my business to you."

"I don't believe I can take a walk with you," Drake answered. "I'm with some friends in there."

He nodded over his shoulder at the door through which he had just come.

"But my business is of a great deal of importance," Dick went on.

"Can't you see me to-morrow?" asked Drake, eager to get back to his companions.

"To-morrow will be altogether too late," Dick replied.

"Then state your business now."

"I'd much rather explain it you as you walk with me," Prescott urged, earnestly.

"Are - are you from the building loan people?" asked Tom Drake, suddenly.

"No, I am not from them," Prescott replied, then added, truthfully enough: "But it's partly about that building loan matter that I wish to talk with you."

"Who sent you here?" asked Drake, half-suspiciously.

"A child," Dick replied. "At least, it was a child's face that gave me the resolution to come here and have a few words with you."

"A child?" repeated Drake. "What child?"

"Yours."

"A child?" echoed the young man. "Mine? Do you mean Mollie?"

"Yes," Dick went on, rapidly. "The child wanted to come here herself to get you, and I came in her stead. It was better that I should come than that little tot.

Don't you think so?"

"I'm afraid I don't understand you," returned Tom Drake, beginning to look offended.

"Mr. Drake, do you know that your wife and child are all dressed up - in their prettiest white gowns, waiting for you to come back to bring them into town to-night for the promised treat? Don't you understand the pain that you're giving them by showing that you prefer a lot of red-nosed loafers in Miller's to your own wife and child? The unhappiness that you're causing them to-night isn't a circumstance to all the misery that you're piling up for them in the years to come. Switch off! Switch off, while you're yet man enough to be able to do it! Won't you do it - please? You must know just how happy that little kid will be when she sees you come swinging down the street to bring her and her mother into town. You know how that little tot's eyes will shine. Can't you hear her saying, `Here's papa! He's come.' Isn't that baby worth a twenty-mile walk for any man to see when he knows she's his own kiddie and waiting for him? Come along, now; they're both waiting for you; they will be the happiest pair you've seen in a long time."

"I don't know but I will toddle along home," said Drake, rather shame-facedly. "I - I didn't realize how time was slipping by. Yes; I guess I'll go home. Much obliged to you for letting me know the time."

But at that moment the door opened, and a voice called out:

"Drake! Oh, Drake. Come here; we want you."

"Can't, now," the young man called back. "I'm due at home."

"Home?" came in two or three jeering voices.

Then several men came out of the saloon, laughing boisterously.

"Come back, Drake! We can't let you slip off like that. You're too good a fellow to play the sneak with us. Come on back!"

"I - I tell you, I'm due at home," insisted Drake, though he spoke more weakly.

"Hey! Here's Drake - says he's going to slip home on us!" called one of the tormentors.

More men came out of the place, some of them staggering. With the new arrivals came one whom Dick and his friends rightly guessed to be Miller - a thickset man, with swaggering manner, insolent expression and rough voice.

"What's this about your going home, Drake?" demanded one of the new arrivals.

"I - I really ought to go home," Drake tried to explain.

"Cut that out," ordered Miller roughly. "You're booked to spend the evening with us, and the evening has hardly begun."

"I promised this young fellow I'd go home," said Drake slowly, "so I guess I will."

"And what has this young feller got to say or do about it?" demanded Miller angrily, as He pushed his way to Drake's side, then glared at Dick Prescott.

"And what have you got to say about his not going home?" Dick asked hotly. "Isn't this a free country, where a man may go home when he chooses?"

"It's a free country, and a man has a right to spend his evening in my place when he's invited," Miller asserted roughly.

"Yes; your invitation will hold until his month's pay is gone from his pocket," Dick flashed back. "That's all you want. Drake has sense enough to see that, and he's leaving you."

"He isn't going home for three hours yet, or anywhere else!" snorted Miller, whose breath proclaimed the fact that he had been using some of his own goods.

Dick laughed contemptuously as he turned to Tom Drake with:

"You see! That fellow thinks he can give you your orders. That fellow begins to believe that he owns you already."

"Who are you calling 'that feller'?" demanded Miller, dropping a heavy hand on Dick's shoulder.

"I referred to you," replied Prescott, pushing the man's hand from his shoulder.

"If you get too funny with me I'll hit you a crack that will carry your head off with it!" snarled the saloon keeper.

"Pshaw!" Prescott answered cuttingly. "You aren't big enough, or man enough, either!"

"What's that?"

Miller aimed a vicious, open-hand blow at young Prescott's face. It didn't land, but, instead, Dick's right hand went up smack! against the fellow's cheek.

"Hang your impudence!" roared Miller, angrily. "I'll pay you for that! I'll teach you!"

He made a rush at Dick, but two men who had been attracted by the commotion jumped in between them.

"Hold on, Miller!" objected one of these passers-by. "You can't pummel a boy!"

"I'll make him howl for hitting me!" roared Miller, doubling his big, powerful fists. "Get out of my way, or I'll run over you!"

"Get out of his way, please!" cried Dick suddenly. "Let Miller at me, if he wants. I'm willing to fight him. I'll fight him for Tom Drake's right to be a man!"

CHAPTER XX

IN THE MILKSOP CLASS?

"Good! And I'll hold the stakes!" cried Tom Reade jovially, as he took light hold of Drake's arm.

"Let Miller at the boy!" howled one of the bystanders. "He'll show the boy something. The kid is getting big enough to learn, and he ought to be taught."

"I'll fight Miller, if he has the sand!" proclaimed Dick, who now had his own reasons for wanting to sting the liquor seller into action. "I'll fight the bully, but not here in a saloon yard. There is a vacant lot the other side of the fence. We'll go in there and see how much of a fighter he is."

More citizens had gathered by this time, and there was every sign of an intention to stop further trouble. But Dave Darrin sprang into the crowd, saying, almost in an undertone:

"The respectable men here don't want to try to stop this affair. A lot of useful manhood depends upon the issue. Don't worry about my friend, if he does look rather young. He can take care of himself, all right, and he is calling for a fight that ought to be fought. You respectable men in the crowd keep still, and just come

H. Irving Hancock

along and see fair play - that's all."

Dave's earnest eloquence won over many of the men representing the better element of the crowd.

"Jove! He's a plucky boy!" cried one man.

"But Miller will pound him to a pulp!"

"Come along, everyone, and see whether rum or water is the best drink for fighting men!" insisted Tom Reade.

There was a general movement toward the vacant lot. Miller was muttering angrily, while some of his red-nosed victims were jeering.

In the field Dick took off his hat and coat, then his tie, and passed them to Dan Dalzell.

"Dave," whispered Prescott, "you stand by as my second, but don't make any too stiff claims of foul. This will have to be rough work, from the start."

Miller, already in his shirt sleeves, did not feel that he had any need of special preparation. Prescott looked altogether too easy. Not that Miller lacked experience in such matters. In other years he had been a prize-fighter of minor rank, and had been considered, in his class, a fairly hard man to beat.

"Now, stand up, boy," ordered the saloon keeper, advancing. "And take back the crack you passed to me."

"Let's have it," taunted Dick, throwing himself on

the defensive.

Miller aimed a vicious blow but did not land. Instead, Prescott hit him on the short ribs.

"If you're going to fight, stand up and take your medicine!" roared Miller, in a rage.

"Handle your own foot-work to suit yourself!" Dick retorted. "I'll do the same. But you can't fight, anyway!"

That taunt threw the liquor seller into a still greater rage. With a yell he sprang at Prescott. But again Dick failed to be there.

The high school boy was not having an easy time, however. Miller's strength was formidable, and Dick knew that he could not stop many straight blows from his opponent without disaster.

Two merely glancing blows scraped the lad, who had landed four blows on Miller. The big fellow, however, seemed able to endure a lot of punishment.

"I didn't come out here to run a race!" Miller insisted, as he tried hard to corner the boy.

"Then stand still, and I won't hit you so hard!" mocked Prescott, as he struck the man again on the short ribs.

Then, of a sudden, Prescott hit the earth. He had miscalculated, and Miller's left fist had landed on his nose.

With a hoarse laugh Miller started to follow up the

advantage with a kick.

"Here! Come back! None of that!" shouted a citizen, throwing his arms around Miller's neck. "Let the boy get to his feet. Fight fair or - we'll lynch you when it's over!"

But Dick was up, the blood flowing freely from his nose. Yet he was hardly less cool as Miller was released and the two again faced each other.

"Finish him up, Miller, and we'll get back to pleasure!" laughed one of the drunkards in maudlin glee.

"The boy has no show. This is an outrage!" protested an indignant citizen. "It ought to be stopped."

As the two sparred Dick suddenly saw his chance to get in under the powerful guard of his antagonist and landed a hard blow on his solar plexus.

"Umph!" grunted Miller, as he partly doubled up under the force of the blow.

That instant was enough for Prescott to drive in a blow that nearly closed one of the big fellow's eyes.

"Stop this fight!" yelled the same citizen.

"Don't you do it!" warned another. "The boy is taking care of himself all right. Let him wind the bruiser up."

Now Miller, smarting and fearing accidental defeat, forgot caution and tried to rush in for a clinch. But this was the kind of attack that Prescott was skilled in dodging.

Dick gave ground before the furious assault, but he did so purposely. Back he went, step by step.

"Miller's got him!" cheered the liquor seller's friends.

At last Dick found what he wanted, the opportunity to drive in again on the big fellow's wind. Miller gave vent to another grunt, followed by a howl, as he felt a stinging fist land against his other eye.

Now, Dick had his man blinded, ready for the finish. A high school fist landed on the side of the big fellow's throat, sending him to his knees. Dick took but half a step backward as he waited for the big fellow to get to his feet. The instant that Miller rose Dick darted in, landing his right fist with all his strength on the tip of the man's chin.

This time the work was complete. Miller went down. Dick, smiling, though breathing quickly, stood over his fallen opponent, counting slowly to ten.

Then, in a moment, those who had favored the boy's side in the fight realized just what had happened.

Loud cheers arose from the crowd. Tom Drake was one of the first to dart in and seize young Prescott's right hand briefly before another man wanted to shake it. Dick was fairly made to run a gauntlet of handshaking.

Most of Miller's "friends" retreated in sulky bad humor. Three of the liquor seller's followers, however, picked the big man up, staggering under his weight, and bore him behind the door that had closed on more than one man's career.

"What do you think of that, Mr. Drake?" demanded Tom Reade jubilantly. "Do you put Dick Prescott in the milk-sop class?"

CHAPTER XXI

THE REVENGE TALK AT MILLER'S

"Let's get out of this place," whispered Dick in Dave's ear as Darry helped him to staunch the flow of blood from his nose.

"There, the bleeding has stopped," muttered Dave. "Now, put on your coat and button it up. Then the blood stains on your shirt won't show."

Tom Drake had very little to say, but he kept close to Prescott.

"Shall we walk down the road a bit, Mr. Drake?" asked Dick, as soon as he had his coat on.

"I'm in a hurry to get home," nodded the young workman. "I shall know where I belong, after this. No more of Miller's for me! For that matter," the young man added, with a hearty laugh, "I don't believe Miller would ever let me in his place again. Of course, in his own mind, he will blame me for what happened to-night."

"I hope he didn't get much of your money before it happened," murmured Prescott, as be and Drake, followed by Dave, Tom and Dan, got clear of the

H. Irving Hancock

crowd and down into a quieter part of the road.

"He got less than a dollar of my wages," replied Drake. "I'm sorry he has that much, but he'll never get any more. Say, Prescott, but you are a fighter! I can imagine how 'sore' Miller will be, to-morrow, over having been whipped by such a stripling as you are."

"I've one great advantage over Miller," Dick rejoined. "I've never tasted alcohol, and Miller has saturated himself with it for years."

"I used to have an idea that liquor was strengthening," murmured Tom Drake. "I know quite a good many men who take it to keep up their strength."

"They're fools, then," Dick retorted tersely. "You could see, in Miller to-night, what alcohol does toward making one strong. That man is still powerful, but I'm satisfied that he was once a great deal stronger. Miller's muscles have grown flabby since he began to drink. His speed is less than it must have been formerly. Even his nerve - his grit - has been impaired by the stuff he has been drinking. Did you notice how early in the fight his wind left him? The man has very little of his former strength, and the blame belongs to the liquor he has used."

"Here's my gate," said Tom Drake, at last, as they halted before the little cottage. "Come in. I've got to tell my wife about you. I wonder where my two girls are?"

Dick and his friends tried to get out of going into the yard, but their new friend would not have it that way, so silently they followed Drake up the path. Then, through a front window, Tom Drake saw his girls.

His wife sat at a table, her head resting on her arms. On the floor sat the toddler, Mollie, still in her white dress. She had two broken dolls, pretending to play with them, but the woebegone look in her little face showed that her thoughts were elsewhere.

Tom Drake choked as he looked in at the window. Then, throwing up his head resolutely, he lifted the latch, entering the room with firm tread.

"I'm a bit late, girls, but come on up in the village!" he invited. "Here, Hattie, you take charge of this little roll," he added, thrusting his money into his wife's hand.

Not more than three minutes later the three Drakes issued from the house, Mollie enjoying a "ride" on her father's shoulder.

"Why, where are the boys?" he demanded. "I left them here."

"Gone, like all good angels, when their work is done," smiled his wife.

"It's all right, anyway, girls," Tom Drake answered cheerily. "We're pretty sure to find 'em up in the village, where we're going."

In the first place that the Drakes entered they came upon Dick and his three friends. The Gridley boys, after dodging a crowd that wanted to lionize young Prescott, had taken refuge, unseen, in the back of an otherwise deserted ice cream saloon.

H. Irving Hancock

"There they are!" cried Mollie, running the length of the shop, as fast as her chubby little legs could take her. She ran straight to Dick who bent over to give her a gentle hug.

"I don't know what to say to you young men," cried Mrs. Drake, halting beside the boys, her voice breaking a little, her eyes moist.

"Then, if you'll permit me to offer a suggestion," Dick smiled back, as he rose, "it seems to me that conversation might spoil several good things. Won't you all sit down and be our guests in a little ice cream feast that we have started?"

It was almost an hour before the little party broke up. A few interested citizens, however, found the hiding place of the Gridley High School boys and insisted on coming in to shake hands with the boys.

"Take your family and slip out through the back door," Dick whispered to Tom Drake.

"I don't know that I'll ever see you again," murmured Drake huskily, "so I want to say -"

"Don't say anything," Dick smiled back. "You're all right, from now on. And we've all learned something to-night. We'll let it rest there. Good-bye, and the best of good luck for you and yours."

So the Drakes escaped from what would have been an embarrassing scene. Nor were Dick and his friends long in getting away from the too-enthusiastic citizens.

"It's late enough for us to go back to camp and turn in,

isn't it?" suggested Tom Reade.

"I was thinking of that myself," Dick admitted.

"You must be tired, anyway," Dave hinted. "You whipped Miller all right, but he was a tiring brute, and I'll wager that you're both sore and exhausted."

"I'll plead guilty to a little bit of both," Dick Prescott assented, laughing at the recollection of Miller at the time when that brute's second eye was closed.

Yet it was more than half an hour after their return to camp when slumber finally began to assert its claim upon the Gridley boys. For Greg and Harry, as soon as they had heard a few words as to the evening's adventure, insisted upon hearing all of it before they would let Dick turn in.

"I'll bet they're sore in Miller's place tonight," chuckled Greg, just before be extinguished the second lantern.

Certainly anger did reign in Miller's place for the rest of that evening.

Miller had been brought to consciousness, after considerable effort. He was even able to be up and about his place, but his swollen features looked like a caricature of a face.

"The schoolboy that was able to do that to you, Miller, must have been eight feet high and as wide as a gate," remarked one of the red-nosed patrons of the place.

"Shut up!" was Miller's gracious response.

There were other drinking places in Fenton, and to these the news of the big fellow's drubbing quickly spread.

Indeed, the fight seemed to be the one topic of the talk of Fenton that evening.

As it happened, it wasn't very long before word was brought to Miller that Dick and his friends were camping down on Andy Hartshorn's place.

"It's queer that Hartshorn will let such young toughs stop on his land!" growled Miller.

"They ought to be chased out of town - that's what!" growled a patron of the place.

More of this talk was heard, until finally someone demanded thickly:

"Well, why can't we chase 'em out of town?"

At first, the idea met with instant favor among the dozen or more worthless men gathered in Miller's saloon. The plan grew in favor until one man, slighter than the rest, observed:

"Say! Stop and think of one thing. We know what one of the boys did to Miller, and there are six of those boys down at the camp!"

That rather cast a damper over the enthusiasm until one blear-eyed man of fifty observed, knowingly:

"Well, we don't need to go alone. There are other men in Fenton who think the way we do. We can go down to the woods in force, and pretend that what we want to do comes as a rebuke administered by the citizens of Fenton."

"Hurrah!" cheered one man who seemed in danger of falling asleep.

"Miller, let us use your telephone," urged the former speaker.

"No, you can't," retorted the liquor seller quickly. "It's all right for you men to do whatever you think is right, but you've got to remember that I've got to be kept out of whatever happens."

Well enough did the wretch know that half-hearted opposition from him would only fan the flame hotter among the men who considered themselves his friends.

So the messengers were sent to the other drinking places in town. Word was passed for a night raid "by representative citizens," as these topers called themselves.

Men of the same turn of mind soon came flocking in from other drinking resorts.

"Don't talk here about what you're going to do for the good of the town," Miller ordered. "Remember, I've got to be kept out of this. My position is a delicate one, you understand."

Soon after midnight the disreputable army of vengeance seekers was straggling down the road. Talking had ceased. These drink-driven wretches were hunting for the camp of Dick & Co. and they were going to attack it in force.

CHAPTER XXII

UNDER THE STING OF THE LASH

When the crowd reached the camp of the high school boys all was silent there. From within the tent came the sounds of the heavy breathing of the sleepers.

"Everything is ready, and there isn't even a dog on the place!" was the exultant word passed back.

"Bunch up! Get in close and surround the tent," ordered another voice. "We want some of you men behind the tent, so that none of the youngsters can slip away from us. Come along, now. Don't talk! Don't make so much noise. Easy, now!"

Thus the figures continued to gather, like so many evil spirits of the night.

Here and there one of the rabble fell over something in the dark, or tripped over a root or stone as he moved about among the shadows.

In the intervals of absolute silence the steady breathing of the six Gridley High School boys could still be heard, until one man in the rabble, less sober than the others, fell over a packing-case, barking his shins and giving vent to a yell of pain.

H. Irving Hancock

"What was that?" asked Greg Holmes, waking and rising on one elbow.

Outside all was quiet again.

"Hey, Dave, get up!" Holmes called, shaking the arm of Darry, who lay asleep on the adjoining cot. "I heard something going on outside. We'll both get up, light a lantern, and -"

"Yes! Get up and come out!" jeered a voice near the tent door. "Come out and have a look at us. The reputable citizens of Fenton are to chase you out of town - and we'll do it, after we get through with teaching you manners!"

"Fellows! Hustle!" shouted Greg, leaping from his cot. "Get ready for trouble. All the topers and loafers who ever knew Miller are outside to avenge the beating that Miller received from Dick!"

"We'll show you!" came a hoarse yell, and then the foremost ruffians in the crowd surged in through the tent door.

But Dave had succeeded in lighting a lantern, and this he took time to hang from a hook on the nearest pole.

Five boys clad only in their pajamas faced this angry rabble. Dan Dalzell slept through the confusion until Reade, in passing him, hauled him from bed.

"What are you men doing here?" thundered Reade, striding to the head of the little group of defenders.

Dick was now beside him like a flash.

"You fellows get out of here!" Prescott ordered, his eyes flaming.

"We'll get out when we get ready!" came the hoarse answer. "Now, friends, show these young imps -"

But that speaker got no further, for a blow from Tom's fist brought him to the ground.

All six of Dick & Co. were now on the fistic firing line.

For a few moments they carried all but consternation to their opponents. As they were forced back from the doorway, however, more and more of the mob poured in.

The very weight of numbers was bound to count against Dick & Co. who were likely to suffer severely at the hands of the miscreants.

Just then there came a flash across the canvas of the tent. The light had been thrown by a swiftly-moving automobile. There was another automobile directly behind it. Both cars came to a stop at the roadside, while from them leaped more than a dozen men.

These men were armed - each with a horsewhip. In an instant the invaders found them selves assailed from behind.

Whish! slash! zip!

In another instant all was uproar. Yells of pain from the mob rent the air, for these latest arrivals were laying about them with their horsewhips with an energy worthy of a good cause.

"Here, you, Andy Hartshorn. Stop that! Don't you hit me! I know you, and I'll have the law on you!" shrieked one of the frightened wretches.

"He who goes to law should have his own hands clean," quoth Farmer Hartshorn, as he dealt the fellow a stinging blow on the legs.

Those of the crowd outside the tent fled in every direction, hotly pursued, and again and again they were stung by the lashes.

Those of the invaders still in the tent were now in a panic to get out and away. As they dashed through the doorway they felt the slashing of horsewhips, while Dick Prescott and his chums hammered them from the rear.

In less than thirty seconds the invaders had been cleared away. They fled in screaming panic, scattering in all directions, some of them being pursued and lashed for a distance of many rods up or down the road.

On all sides the fleeing wretches threatened their persecutors with the law, but these threats did not stop the punishment.

"I guess it's all right now, boys!" called Farmer Hartshorn grimly, as he strode up to the place where Dick & Co. had gathered just beyond their tent.

"What was that mob, anyway?" Dick asked.

"A gang that came after revenge for what you did to Miller to-night," laughed the farmer.

"I thought as much," muttered Dick.

"They've been gathering at Miller's, and other like places, for a couple of hours," Mr. Hartshorn went on. "But, as is the case with all such movements, some news of it leaked outside. We got word a bit late, or we'd have been here before that crowd came along. When we knew the word was straight some of us telephoned to others, and our crowd was gotten together, but as it is, we got here in season. Are any of you boys hurt?"

"No, sir; not one of us," Dick declared. "But some of us might have been seriously injured if you gentlemen had been delayed for another minute."

"We'll know the rascals to-morrow," spoke up another of the rescuers. "If they appear on the streets at all they'll be recognized. We have marked them up pretty well. They've gone off vowing to have the law on us."

"All they'll do will be to put arnica on themselves," declared Mr. Hartshorn. "And they will send friends to the drugstore for the arnica. They won't take the risk of being recognized on the streets. They'll be a shame-faced lot in the morning."

"It was mighty good of you men to come down and help us out," murmured Dick Prescott gratefully. "We would have had a pretty tough time if we had been left to ourselves."

"We'd go further than we've traveled tonight, to help

out boys like you," declared another man present. "Prescott, that was a fine thing you did to Miller tonight, and Tom Drake will be grateful as long as he lives."

"If Drake keeps away from drink in the future," Dick answered, "he will have reason to congratulate himself."

"Oh, Drake will keep away from the stuff after this," said one of the citizens. "Young Drake has a head of his own, and we'll see that he uses it. We'll keep a friendly eye over him. Don't worry. Young Tom Drake will never associate with any of Miller's kind again."

"Whenever any of you boys want to go to sleep, just say so," urged Mr. Hartshorn, "and we'll run along."

"Why, I believe we're a bit waked up, at present," smiled young Prescott, as he turned to glance at the others in the light thrown by the automobile lamps.

"I don't feel as though I needed any more sleep," laughed Tom Reade.

"If you boys are thinking of sitting up to watch against another surprise, don't bother about it," advised Mr. Hartshorn. "You've seen the very last that you'll see of those rascals. Men of that sort never have nerve enough to attempt a risky thing twice."

"I'm going to put some wood in the stove and make coffee," Danny Grin announced.

"Can't we offer you a cup of coffee, gentlemen?" proposed Prescott. "And sandwiches? We have plenty of the fixings for sandwiches."

The idea prevailed to such an extent that Dalzell put on a kettle of water to boil, while Tom and Dave began to slice bread and open tinned meats.

"I'm going to sit down on the ground and be comfortable," declared one of the Fentonites, when coffee and food were passed around.

"Do you know, gentlemen," said Tom Reade, as he munched a sandwich, "I'm beginning to like Fenton next to our own town of Gridley."

"Fenton isn't anywhere near as large a place as Gridley," replied one of the guests.

"No; but for its size Fenton is a lively place," Reade went on. "There seems to be something happening here every minute."

"That is when young fellows like you come along and start the ball rolling," chuckled Farmer Hartshorn. "There has been more excitement to-night in Fenton than I can remember during the last five years. I've seen you play football, Prescott, and you're a wonder at the game. Yet what you did to-night for young Tom Drake is a bigger thing than winning a whole string of the greatest football games of the year."

"Football is more exciting, though," smiled Dick.

"Is it?" demanded Mr. Hartshorn. "More exciting than what you've been through tonight? Then I'll never play football! More excitement than you've had to-night isn't healthful for any growing young fellow!"

For fully an hour these men of Fenton remained at the camp, talking with their young hosts, and, incidentally, picking up a lot of information about the sports and pastimes that most interest wide-awake boys of to-day.

At last, however, disclaiming the thanks offered by Dick & Co., the guests went away in the automobiles that had brought them, while Dick Prescott and his chums prepared to finish out the night's rest.

CHAPTER XXIII

TIMMY, THE GENTLEMAN, AT HOME

"Oh, won't life seem stale when we get back into the land of crowded business streets and schoolhouses?" grumbled Reade, as, perched on the seat of the camp wagon, he drove out onto the highway the next morning, followed by the other members of Dick & Co. on foot.

"No, sir!" Darry retorted. "Life won't seem stale on that account. Instead, it will be brightened by the pleasant recollection of this summer's fun, which is now so soon to be ended."

"You're not going through Fenton, are you, Dick?" asked Greg.

"I guess we'll have to. We were pretty well cleaned out of some of our provisions last night. We shall have to replenish our food supply, and Fenton is the only real town along our route to-day. The rest are small farming villages."

"But we'll attract a lot of attention," declared Holmes.

"You won't," laughed Darry. "You didn't go to town with us last night, and consequently you're not known there."

"I'd rather not go through the town myself," Dick explained, "but it seems to me that as long as we must purchase supplies we ought to make a stop in the town that's likely to have the best stores."

Fenton's principal street had rather a sleepy look this hot August morning. There were but few people abroad as Dick & Co. turned into the main thoroughfare.

At Miller's place there was not a sign of life. "I'll wager that brute is applying raw beef to his eyes this morning," muttered Tom, somewhat vindictively.

Prescott's watchful glance soon discovered a provision store that looked more than usually promising. At a word from him Tom reined in the horse, while Prescott and Darrin went inside to make purchases.

When they came out they found Farmer Hartshorn and another man talking with Tom Reade.

"You young men of Gridley don't look any the worse, this morning, for the excitement you had last night," said Mr. Hartshorn, after a cordial greeting. "Reade tells me that you left the milk-pail at my house as you came along."

"Yes, sir," Dick nodded. "And with it, we left our very best thanks for the fine treat that milk proved to be to us."

"Prescott, shake hands with Mr. Stark. He's our leading lawyer in this little place."

"I've heard a good deal about you this morning," said the lawyer, as he shook hands.

Mr. Stark was a tall, thin man, of perhaps forty-five years of age. Warm as was the day he was attired wholly in black, a bit rusty, and wore a high silk hat that was beginning to show signs of age. He belonged to a type of rural lawyer that is now passing.

"I think we've heard of you, too," smiled Prescott innocently.

"Have you?" asked the lawyer, looking somewhat astonished.

"Yes," Dick went on. "I think it must have been your letter that Mr. Reuben Hinman showed us one day. It was in regard to a bill he had given you to collect. Mr. Hinman is in the hospital and must need quite a bit of money just at present so I beg to express the hope that you have been able to collect the other half of the debt - the half that belongs to him."

Lawyer Stark reddened a good deal, despite his sallow skin.

"Why, what about that other half? What's the story?" questioned Mr. Hartshorn, his eyes, twinkling as though he scented something amusing.

"Oh - er - just a matter of business between a client and myself," the lawyer explained, in some confusion.

"And poor old Hinman was the client, eh?" asked the farmer.

"We don't know very much about the matter," Dave Darrin broke in, a trifle maliciously, for he fell that it might be a good thing to show up this lawyer's tricky work. "Mr. Hinman gave Mr. Stark a bill of twenty dollars to collect, and -"

"It was - er - all a matter of business between a client and myself, and therefore of a confidential nature," Lawyer Stark broke in, reddening still more.

But Dave was in no mood, just then, to be headed off so easily, so he went on:

"Mr. Hinman showed us the letter, and asked us what we thought of it, so that rather broke the confidential nature of the matter. You see," turning to Mr. Hartshorn, "the bill was for twenty dollars, and it seems that. Mr. Stark was to have half for his trouble in collecting it. Now the letter that Mr. Hinman showed us -"

"I protest, young man!" exclaimed the lawyer.

"The letter," Darry went on calmly, "was to the effect that Mr. Stark had collected his own half of the twenty dollars, and that the collection of Mr. Hinman's half of the money seemed doubtful."

"Now, now, Stark!" exclaimed the farmer, looking sharply at the lawyer. "Surely, that isn't your way of doing business with a poor and aged client like Hinman!"

"I have collected the remainder of the bill, and am going to mail a settlement to Mr. Hinman to-day," muttered the lawyer, trying to look unconcerned. "All just a matter of routine office business, Mr. Hartshorn."

But the lawyer felt wholly uncomfortable. He was thinking, at that moment, that he would heartily enjoy kicking Darrin if the latter didn't look so utterly healthy and uncommonly able to take care of himself.

"Do I hear you discussing money that is due my father?" inquired a voice behind them. "If so, my father is very ill, as you doubtless know, and I would take pleasure in receiving the money on his behalf."

Timothy Hinman, looking wholly the man of fashion, made this offer. He had come up behind the group, and there was a look in his eyes which seemed to say that the handling of some of the family money would not be distasteful to him just then.

"I'll walk along with you to your office, Mr. Stark, and receipt for the money, if you're headed that way," suggested the younger Hinman again.

"Unless you hold a regular power of attorney from your father, you could hardly give me a valid receipt," replied the lawyer sourly, as he turned away from Mr. Hartshorn and the boys and started down the street.

"Won't my receipt do until my father is up and about once more?" pressed Timothy Hinman.

"No, sir; it won't," snapped the lawyer.

"Have you heard, this morning, how your father is?" Dick inquired.

"Just heard, at the post-office," Hinman answered. "My father had a very bad day yesterday. Er - in fact, the chances, I am sorry to say, appear to be very much against his recovery."

"He must feel the strain of his father's illness," observed Dave sarcastically.

"He does!" retorted Mr. Hartshorn, with emphasis. "If old Reuben dies young Timothy must go to work for a living. The disgrace of toil will almost kill him. His two sisters are as bad as he is. They've never done a stroke of work, either. All three have lived on the poor old peddler's earnings all their lives, though not one of the three would be willing to keep the old man's house for him. There are a lot of sons and daughters like them to-day. Perhaps there always have been."

Mr. Hartshorn waited until Dick and Dave had finished with the purchases and had loaded them on the wagon.

Then the farmer shook hands with each member of Dick & Co.

"I'm coming up to Gridley to see the football game this Thanksgiving," he promised. "I hope I'll see as good a game as I did last year. Anyway, I'll see the work of a mighty fine lot of young fellows."

Prescott expressed again the heartiest thanks of himself and friends for the timely aid given them during the trouble in camp.

"We've lost so much time this morning that we'll have to hustle for the rest of the day," Tom called down from the wagon seat, as he started the horse.

An hour later they were more than three miles past Fenton.

"Get out of the way, Tom!" called Dave. "Drive up into someone's yard like lightning. Here comes a whizz wagon that wants the whole highway."

Behind them, its metal trimmings flashing in the sun, and leaving a trail of dust in its wake, came an automobile traveling at least sixty miles an hour.

Yet, fast as the car was going when it passed them, the speed did not prevent one occupant from recognizing them and calling out derisively. Then, half a mile ahead, the car stopped, turned, and came slowly back toward the wondering Gridley boys.

CHAPTER XXIV

CONCLUSION

Five rather contemptuous pairs of youthful eyes surveyed Dick & Co. as their outfit plodded on its way.

"Aren't they a mucker looking outfit?" demanded one voice from the car.

Then the automobile shot ahead again.

"Phin Drayne! Humph!" said Darry rather scornfully.

Phin Drayne is no stranger to the readers of the "*High School Boys Series*," who will recall Phin as the "kicker" who, at the game on the Thanksgiving before, had sulked and refused to go on the field, hoping to induce the other members of the Gridley High School gridiron team to coax him to play. Thus Dick, though suffering at that time from injuries, and forbidden to play, had been forced out onto the field to help win the great game of the season. Of course a kicker like Drayne did not like Prescott. Dick worried but little on that account.

"There! they are coming back," Greg announced. "They are grinning at us again."

"If they keep on grinning," threatened Darry, "we'll sic Danny Grin onto them. When it comes to grinning our own Danny boy can grin down anything on earth."

As if to verify that claim, Dalzell began to grin broadly. Besides this, he turned his face toward the occupants of the automobile as it once more passed Dick & Co.

Just at this point the car slowed down. Phin Drayne looked as though he were exhibiting his fellow students of Gridley High School as so many laughable freaks.

"That's what I call a vacation on the cheap," Drayne remarked to his friends, in a tone wholly audible to Dick & Co.

"It is 'on the cheap,'" Dick called out pleasantly. "And yet, our trip hasn't been such a very cheap one, either, and we've earned all the money ourselves. I don't suppose, Drayne, you ever earned as much money in your life."

"I don't have to," scoffed Phin Drayne. "My father is able to supply me with whatever money I need."

"Why!" uttered Dan Dalzell. "Our old Drayne is just another Timmy Hinman of the regular kind, isn't he?"

Dan looked so comical when he made this observation that his five chums burst into a shout of gleeful laughter.

Phin Drayne didn't relish that very sincere laughter. Though he didn't understand the allusion, he suspected that he was being made the butt of a joke by Dick & Co.

"Drive on, George," he requested his friend at the wheel. "One hates to be seen in the company of such fellows."

The car's speed was let out several notches, and shot down the road ahead of Dick & Co.'s plain little caravan.

"Now that I think of it," Dick declared, "Phin is just another edition of Timmy Hinman, isn't he? And so are quite a good many of the fellows we know. The world must be nearly as full of Timmy Hinmans as it is of fathers either wealthy or well-to-do. I'd hate to belong to the Timmy Hinman crowd!"

"As for me," sighed Tom comically, "I don't see any chance of my becoming a Timmy until I'm able to do it on money accumulated for myself."

As Phin Drayne was still in Gridley High School, and had an overweening idea of himself as a football player, it is extremely likely that we shall hear of him again, for which reason, if for no other, we may as well dismiss him from these present pages.

A few more days of earnest hiking, followed by restful sleep in camp at night, brought Dick & Co., one fine afternoon toward the end of August, in sight of the spires of Gridley.

"There's the good old town!" called Dick, first to reach the rise of ground from which the view of Gridley was to be had.

"Good old town, indeed!" glowed Dave Darrin.

"Whoop!" shouted Tom Reade irrepressibly. "Whoop! And then - whoop!"

Dalzell, as he stood still for a few moments, gazing ahead, grinned broadly.

"He thinks his native town is a joke!" called Greg Holmes reproachfully.

"No," replied Dalzell, with a solemn shake of his head. "I am the joke, and it's on Gridley for being my native town."

"I'm glad to be back - when I get there," announced Hazy. "I shall be glad, even if for nothing more than the chance to rest my feet."

"Nonsense!" Dick retorted. "You'll be out on Main Street, to-night, ready to tramp miles and miles, if anything amusing turns up."

At the first shade by the roadside Dick &. Co. halted for fifteen minutes to rest.

"Now, each one of you do a little silent thinking," Prescott urged.

"Give us the topic, then," proposed Reade.

"Fellows," Dick went on, mounting a stump and thrusting one hand inside his flannel shirt, in imitation of the pose of an orator, "the next year will be an eventful one for all of us. In that time we shall wind up our courses at the Gridley High School. From the day that we set forth from Gridley High School we shall be actively at work creating our careers. We are destined to become great men, everyone of us!"

"Tell that to the Senate!" mocked Tom Reade.

"Well, then," Dick went on, accepting the doubt of their future greatness, "we shall, at least, if we are worth our salt, become useful men in the world, and I don't know but that is very close to being great. For the man who isn't useful in the world has no excuse for living. Now, in a little more than another hour, we shall be treading the pavements of good old Gridley. Let us do it with a sense of triumph."

"Triumph?" quizzed Tom soberly. "What about?"

"The sense of triumph," Dick retorted, "will arise from the fact that this is to be the last and biggest year in which we are to give ourselves the final preparation for becoming either great or useful men. I'm not going to say any more on this subject. Perhaps you fellows think I've been talking nonsense on purpose. I haven't. Neither have I tried to preach to you, for preaching is out of my line. But, fellows, I hope you all feel, as solemnly as I do myself, just what this next year must mean to us in work, in study - in a word, in achievement. It won't do any of us any harm, once in a while to feel solemn, for five seconds at a time, over what we are going to do this year to assure our futures."

For once Tom Reade didn't have a jest ready. For once Dalzell forgot to grin.

The march was taken up again. The next halt was made

in Gridley, thus ending their long training hike, the boys going to their respective homes.

"Just give three silent cheers, and we won't startle anyone," Tom proposed.

"We went out on the trip to harden ourselves," murmured Dave, "and I must admit that we have all done it."

That evening Dick and Harry Hazelton drove the horse and wagon over to Tottenville, where the camp wagon was returned to its owner, Mr. Newbegin Titmouse.

"You young men have worn this wagon quite: a bit," whined Mr. Titmouse, after he had painstakingly inspected the wagon by the light of a lantern.

"I think we've brought it back in fine condition, sir," replied Dick, and he spoke the truth. "The wagon looks better, Mr. Titmouse, than you had expected to see it."

"You owe me about five dollars for extra wear and tear," insisted the money-loving Mr. Titmouse.

But he didn't get the money. Again Dick Prescott turned out to be an excellent business man. Dick was most courteous, but he refuted all of Mr. Titmouse's claims for extra payment, in the end even such a money-grubber as Mr. Newbegin Titmouse gave up the effort to extort more money for the use of his wagon than was his due. He even used his lantern to light the boys through the dark side alley to the street where the trolley car ran.

Two or three times after this Dick and his friends heard

from Tom Drake. That young workman never repeated his earlier error. In time he paid for his home, then began the saving of money for other purposes. To-day Drake owns his own machine shop and is highly prosperous.

Old Reuben Hinman lingered many days between life and death. At last he recovered, and in time was discharged from the hospital.

However, his first attempts to run the peddler's wagon again revealed the fact that the peddler's days on the road were over. He was no longer strong enough for the hard outdoor life.

Timothy Hinman and his sisters came forward when the Overseers of the Poor began to look into the peddler's affairs. These dutiful children wanted to be sure to obtain whatever might be their share of their father's belongings.

Timothy and his sisters obtained their full shares - nothing.

The Overseers of the Poor found that they could effect an arrangement by which the peddler's home, his horse and wagon, stock and good will could be sold for four thousand dollars.

This was done. With half the money Reuben Hinman was able to purchase his way into a home for old men. Here he will be maintained, without further expense, as long as he lives, and he will live in a degree of comfort amounting, with this simple-minded ex-peddler, to positive luxury.

The other two thousand dollars, at the suggestion of the Overseers of the Poor, was spent in buying an annuity from a life insurance company. This annuity provides ample spending money for Reuben Hinman whenever, in fine weather, he wishes to go forth from the home and enjoy himself in the world at large.

Timothy has been forced to go to work as a valet. The daughters tearfully support themselves as milliners. Reuben Hinman long ago spent the ten dollars received from Lawyer Stark.

The tramp who accepted work from Dr. Hewitt made good in every sense of the word. In fact he did so well that, in time, he took unto himself a wife and is now the head of a family, which lives in a little cottage built on Dr. Hewitt's estate. The name of "Jim Joggers" has given way to the real name of that former knight of the road. However, as the man is sensitive about his idle past, we prefer to remember him as "Joggers."

And now we come to the end of the "*High School Boys Vacation Series.*"

It is to be hoped that these four little volumes have not dwelt so much upon fun as to make it appear that pleasure is all there is in the world that is worth while.

Dick Prescott and his friends were destined to discover that all the pleasure in the world that is worth anything at all comes only as the reward of continuous, hard and useful endeavor.

The further adventures that befell Dick Prescott and his chums while they were still Gridley High School boys will be found in the fourth volume of the "*High School*

H. Irving Hancock

Boys Series," which is published under the title, "*The High School Captain of the Team; Or, Dick & Co. Leading the Athletic Vanguard.*"

In that volume, the last dealing with Dick Prescott's high school days, the value of sports and the worth of honor and faithful work will be set forth as strongly as lies within the power of the narrator of these events.

Choose from Thousands of 1stWorldLibrary Classics By

Adolphus WilliamWard
Aesop
Agatha Christie
Alexander Aaronsohn
Alexander Kielland
Alexandre Dumas
Alfred Gatty
Alfred Ollivant
Alice Duer Miller
Alice Turner Curtis
Alice Dunbar
Ambrose Bierce
Amelia E. Barr
Andrew Lang
Andrew McFarland Davis
Anna Sewell
Annie Besant
Annie Hamilton Donnell
Annie Payson Call
Anton Chekhov
Arnold Bennett
Arthur Conan Doyle
Arthur Ransome
Atticus
B. M. Bower
Basil King
Bayard Taylor
Ben Macomber
Booth Tarkington
Bram Stoker
C. Collodi
C. E. Orr
C. M. Ingleby
Carolyn Wells
Catherine Parr Traill
Charles A. Eastman
Charles Dickens
Charles Dudley Warner
Charles Farrar Browne
Charles Ives
Charles Kingsley
Charles Lathrop Pack
Charles Whibley
Charles Willing Beale
Charlotte M. Braeme
Charlotte M.Yonge
Clair W. Hayes
Clarence Day Jr.
Clarence E. Mulford

Clemence Housman
Confucius
Cornelis DeWitt Wilcox
Cyril Burleigh
D. H. Lawrence
Daniel Defoe
David Garnett
Don Carlos Janes
Donald Keyhole
Dorothy Kilner
Dougan Clark
E. Nesbit
E.P.Roe
E. Phillips Oppenheim
Edgar Allan Poe
Edgar Rice Burroughs
Edith Wharton
Edward J. O'Biren
John Cournos
Edwin L. Arnold
Eleanor Atkins
Elizabeth Cleghorn
Gaskell
Elizabeth Von Arnim
Ellem Key
Emily Dickinson
Erasmus W. Jones
Ernie Howard Pie
Ethel Turner
Ethel Watts Mumford
Eugenie Foa
Eugene Wood
Evelyn Everett-Green
Everard Cotes
F. J. Cross
Federick Austin Ogg
Ferdinand Ossendowski
Francis Bacon
Francis Darwin
Frances Hodgson Burnett
Frank Gee Patchin
Frank Harris
Frank Jewett Mather
Frank L. Packard
Frederick Trevor Hill
Frederick Winslow Taylor
Friedrich Kerst
Friedrich Nietzsche
Fyodor Dostoyevsky

Gabrielle E. Jackson
Garrett P. Serviss
Gaston Leroux
George Ade
Geroge Bernard Shaw
George Ebers
George Eliot
George MacDonald
George Orwell
George Tucker
George W. Cable
George Wharton James
Gertrude Atherton
Grace E. King
Grant Allen
Guillermo A. Sherwell
Gulielma Zollinger
Gustav Flaubert
H. A. Cody
H. B. Irving
H. G. Wells
H. H. Munro
H. Irving Hancock
H. Rider Haggard
H. W. C. Davis
Hamilton Wright Mabie
Hans Christian Andersen
Harold Avery
Harold McGrath
Harriet Beecher Stowe
Harry Houidini
Helent Hunt Jackson
Helen Nicolay
Hendy David Thoreau
Henrik Ibsen
Henry Adams
Henry Ford
Henry Frost
Henry James
Henry Jones Ford
Henry Seton Merriman
Henry Wadsworth
Longfellow
Henry W Longfellow
Herbert A. Giles
Herbert N. Casson
Herman Hesse
Homer
Honore De Balzac

Horace Walpole
Horatio Alger, Jr.
Howard Pyle
Howard R. Garis
Hugh Lofting
Hugh Walpole
Humphry Ward
Ian Maclaren
Israel Abrahams
J.G.Austin
J. Henri Fabre
J. M. Barrie
J. Macdonald Oxley
J. S. Knowles
J. Storer Clouston
Jack London
Jacob Abbott
James Allen
James Lane Allen
James Andrews
James Baldwin
James DeMille
James Joyce
James Oliver Curwood
James Oppenheim
James Otis
Jane Austen
Jens Peter Jacobsen
Jerome K. Jerome
John Burroughs
John F. Kennedy
John Gay
John Glasworthy
John Habberton
John Joy Bell
John Milton
John Philip Sousa
Jonathan Swift
Joseph Carey
Joseph Conrad
Joseph Jacobs
Julian Hawthrone
Julies Vernes
Justin Huntly McCarthy
Kakuzo Okakura
Kenneth Grahame
Kate Langley Bosher
L. A. Abbot
L. T. Meade
L. Frank Baum
Laura Lee Hope

Laurence Housman
Leo Tolstoy
Leonid Andreyev
Lewis Carroll
Lilian Bell
Lloyd Osbourne
Louis Tracy
Louisa May Alcott
Lucy Fitch Perkins
Lucy Maud Montgomery
Lydia Miller Middleton
Lyndon Orr
M. H. Adams
Margaret E. Sangster
Margaret Vandercook
Maria Edgeworth
Maria Thompson Daviess
Mariano Azuela
Marion Polk Angellotti
Mark Overton
Mark Twain
Mary Austin
Mary Cole
Mary Rowlandson
Mary Wollstonecraft
Shelley
Max Beerbohm
Myra Kelly
Nathaniel Hawthrone
O. F. Walton
Oscar Wilde
Owen Johnson
P.G.Wodehouse
Paul and Mable Thorn
Paul G. Tomlinson
Paul Severing
Peter B. Kyne
Plato
R. Derby Holmes
R. L. Stevenson
Rabindranath Tagore
Rahul Alvares
Ralph Waldo Emmerson
Rene Descartes
Rex E. Beach
Richard Harding Davis
Richard Jefferies
Robert Barr
Robert Frost
Robert Gordon Anderson
Robert L. Drake

Robert Lansing
Robert Michael Ballantyne
Robert W. Chambers
Rosa Nouchette Carey
Ross Kay
Rudyard Kipling
Samuel B. Allison
Samuel Hopkins Adams
Sarah Bernhardt
Selma Lagerlof
Sherwood Anderson
Sigmund Freud
Standish O'Grady
Stanley Weyman
Stella Benson
Stephen Crane
Stewart Edward White
Stijn Streuvels
Swami Abhedananda
Swami Parmananda
T. S. Ackland
The Princess Der Ling
Thomas A. Janvier
Thomas A Kempis
Thomas Anderton
Thomas Bailey Aldrich
Thomas Bulfinch
Thomas De Quincey
Thomas H. Huxley
Thomas Hardy
Thomas More
Thornton W. Burgess
U. S. Grant
Valentine Williams
Victor Appleton
Virginia Woolf
Walter Scott
Washington Irving
Wilbur Lawton
Wilkie Collins
Willa Cather
Willard F. Baker
William Makepeace
Thackeray
William W. Walter
Winston Churchill
Yei Theodora Ozaki
Young E. Allison
Zane Grey

www.ingramcontent.com/pod-product-compliance
Lightning Source LLC
Chambersburg PA
CBHW050035180626
46810CB00002B/730